"The gatekeeper recognized him and the gate fell away. The Shepherd put his ax and his crook into the bag at his belt and stepped out onto the bridge. As always he felt a rush of vertigo as he walked the narrow arch over the foaming acid of the moat. Then he was across and striding down the road to the village.

A child was playing with a dog on a grassy hillside. The Shepherd looked up at him, his fine dark face made bright by his eyes. The boy shrank back, and the Shepherd heard a woman's voice cry out, "Back here, Derry, you fool!" The Shepherd walked on down the road as the boy retreated among the hayricks on the far slope. The Shepherd could hear the scolding, "Play near the castle again, and he'll make kingsmeat of you."

Kingsmeat, thought the Shepherd. How the king does get hungry. The word had come down through the quick grapevine—steward to cook to captain to guard to shepherd and then he was dressed and out the door only minutes after the king had muttered, "For supper, what is your taste?" and the queen had fluttered all her arms and said, "Not stew again, I hope."

And now the Shepherd was out to harvest from the flock.

from *Kingsmeat*

Tor Books by Orson Scott Card

The Folk of the Fringe
Future on Fire (editor)
Future on Ice (editor)*
Hart's Hope
Saints
Songmaster
The Worthing Saga
Wyrms

The Tales of Alvin Maker
Seventh Son
Red Prophet
Prentice Alvin

Ender
Ender's Game
Speaker for the Dead
Xenocide

Homecoming
The Memory of Earth
The Call of Earth

Short Fiction
Maps in a Mirror:
The Short Fiction of Orson Scott Card (hardcover)
Maps in a Mirror, Volume 1: The Changed Man (paperback)
Maps in a Mirror, Volume 2: Flux (paperback)
Maps in a Mirror, Volume 3: Cruel Miracles (paperback)
Maps in a Mirror, Volume 4: Monkey Sonatas (paperback)*

*forthcoming

CRUEL MIRACLES

ORSON SCOTT CARD

A TOM DOHERTY ASSOCIATES BOOK
NEW YORK

CRUEL MIRACLES

Copyright © 1990 by Orson Scott Card

Previously published as book four of *Maps in a Mirror* by Orson Scott Card (Tor, 1990)

All rights reserved, including the right to reproduce this book, or portions thereof, in any form.

Cover art by Peter Scanlan

A Tor Book
Published by Tom Doherty Associates, Inc.
175 Fifth Avenue
New York, N.Y. 10010

Tor ® is a registered trademark of Tom Doherty Associates, Inc.

ISBN: 0-812-52304-0

First edition: December 1992

Printed in the United States of America

0 9 8 7 6 5 4 3 2

**To Charlie Ben,
who can fly**

CONTENTS

CRUEL MIRACLES

INTRODUCTION

I BELIEVE THAT speculative fiction—science fiction in particular—is the last American refuge of religious literature.

An odd thing to say, it might seem, particularly since science fiction openly requires that gods be either absent or explained. The moment you have a character pray and get an answer that is *not* explained through perfectly natural phenomena, the story ceases to be publishable as science fiction. In Stephen King's *The Stand*, which began as science fiction—an escaped virus destroys almost all of humanity—some characters' mystical dreams could perhaps have been acceptable as science fiction, because the Jungian collective unconscious has won a grudging place as legitimate grist for the sf mill. But when, at the end, the finger of God comes down out of heaven and blows up Walking Man's nuclear missile—well, that crossed the line, and *The Stand* was clearly either fantasy or religious literature.

It would be fantasy if the god that acted were a god that the readers were not expected to believe in their real lives. It would be religious literature if the readers were expected to believe that such divine interventions actually *do* happen in reality. But no way in hell is the story going to stand up as science fiction if gods are both supernatural and real in the world of the tale.

So why do I call science fiction the last bastion of American religious literature?

You have to understand that what passes for religious literature in the U.S. today is really *inspirational* literature. The Religious, New Age, and Occult publishing categories all contain very similar kinds of stories: Isn't it wonderful that we understand the truth and live the right way, and ain't it a shame about the poor saps who don't. Their fiction (when they have fiction at all) is self-congratulatory. It doesn't explore, it merely affirms. It gives readers an emotional high in connection with membership in their own community of faith.

Real religious literature, I think, does something entirely different. It explores the nature of the universe and discovers the purpose behind it. When we find that purpose, we have found God, because in all religions at all times, regardless of the outward descriptions of God or gods, deity serves the same role: He (or she or they) is the purposer, the planner. And human beings, either with or without their knowledge or consent (depending on one's theology), are following that plan.

I think existential literature still falls into this category, for even though, after much searching, characters always discover that there is no God and therefore no purpose, the story is nevertheless about the need and search for purpose, and the climax is the discovery of the absence of one. Stories about God's nonexistence are still about God, and therefore are still a branch of religious literature.

The need to discover purpose in our lives is a universal human hunger. Even the slimiest, most evil people alive try to find meaning in their self-gratification; and the best of people shunt others' praise from themselves by ascribing their works to the purposes of a higher being.

There is a tendency, though, in the "true" stories available today to explain human behavior, to remove purpose—motive—from serious consideration. We tend to accept the notion that mechanical, not purposive, causation accounts for the things people do. Joe Sinister is a criminal because his parents beat him or because of a chemical imbalance in his brain or because of a genetic disorder that removed the function we call conscience. Jane Dexter, on the other hand, acts altruistically because she is compensating for feelings of inadequacy or because she has a brain disorder that causes an overactive sense of responsibility.

These explanations of human behavior may be

accurate; I'm interested in the question, but the issue of accuracy is, in fact, quite irrelevant to human societies. A human community that uses mechanical causation to account for human behavior *cannot survive,* because it cannot hold its members accountable for their behavior. That is, no matter how you account for the origin of a human behavior, a community must continue to judge the perpetrator on the basis of his intent, as near as that intent can be understood (or guessed, or assumed). That is why parents inevitably ask their children the unanswerable question: Why did you do that? Terrible as that question is, it at least puts the responsibility back on the child's head and forces the child to ask himself the question that society absolutely requires him to answer: Why do I do the things I do? And how, by changing my motives, can I change my behavior? Whereas nothing is more debilitating or enervating for a child than parents who do not ask why, but rather say, You're just going through a phase, or, You can't help that, or I understand that's just the way you are. Such a child, if he believes these stories, has no hope of getting control of himself and therefore no hope of becoming an adult, responsible citizen of the community. We must believe in motives for human behavior, or we cannot maintain community life.

And once we have embarked on that course—judging each other by motive rather than explaining behavior by mechanical causation alone—the fundamental religious question of the meaning or purpose of life cannot be avoided.

What *can* be avoided is the question of whether there is an ultimate purposer whose plan we all fulfill—and most American fiction does avoid it, including almost all of the stories published within the category labeled Religious Literature. Instead, purpose or lack of it is assumed.

Not, however, in science fiction. There alone we find the search for the purposer is still alive. Indeed, in story after story the question arises and is explored at depths that would be impossible in any other genre—even fantasy. For while fantasy is uniquely suited to dealing with human universals—the mythic—science fiction is uniquely suited to dealing with suprahuman universals—the metaphysical. Fantasy can hardly deal seriously with gods, because gods are common motifs, like magic swords and unicorns. Readers aren't expected to *believe* in them. (Few things are more jarring to a fantasy writer than to meet a reader who actually believes in those fantasy worlds. The dowsers and seventh sons who wrote to me or telephoned me after my Alvin Maker series started appearing finally led me to stop listing my address in the phone book. I didn't want these people to know where I lived.) But because science fiction specifically excludes supernatural gods as characters in stories, it is possible for science fiction to explore the purpose of life deeply and thoroughly without being distracted by existing theologies.

One of the best examples is in the work of Isaac Asimov. The good doctor has made it clear over the years that he has no belief in any kind of transcendent god, and his work bears this out. But his novels are almost all profoundly religious in the sense that they invariably affirm both the need for and the existence of a purposer. The original Foundation trilogy is explicitly about Hari Seldon's plan and purpose for humanity, and how it worked regardless of the conscious intent of the leaders of Terminus. And, when the plan seemed thwarted by an unplanned-for intruder, the mutant Mule, we find that there is a Second Foundation, which continues to fill Seldon's role, ongoing purposers and planners guiding the destiny of humankind. Furthermore, they realize they can't possibly do their work if humankind is aware of their presence—their scientific planning can't function unless it is not known to function. Therefore they have to fake their own destruction. The nontranscendent god of Asimov's fiction must remain invisible and ineffable—must remain, in fact, rather transcendent.

What shows up in Asimov shows up elsewhere as well. Gene Wolfe's novels are quite explicitly religious—more so than Tolkien's *Lord of the Rings*, which is a profoundly religious (and, in fact, Catholic) work. Frank Herbert's *Dune* and its sequels are even more obvious. Lisa Goldstein's *Tourists* and *A Mask for the General* both reveal, at the end, the active role of some purposer in making things work out according to a certain pattern in spite of the weakness of the leading characters—though in her cosmology, unlike Stephen King's, the voluntary actions of human beings *do* play a vital role in their salvation, a very non-Calvinist view of the relationship between man and the universal purposer.

Certainly there are many more; equally certain is the fact that many, perhaps most, science fiction novels *don't* deal with the plan of life and its planner. Nor is this subject unheard-of in works outside of science fiction. My point is that in science fiction, the relationship between man and god can be dealt with explicitly, in depth, and with great originality, without necessarily being connected to any religious system that has ever existed on Earth. Indeed, whenever science fiction touches on actual contemporary religions, it is almost always hostile to them. Yet it deals with religious *ideas* in a way almost not seen in serious American fiction outside of sci-fi.

So far I have referred to other writers' work; my own is also religious, in exactly this fashion—and in another, which I will deal with soon. But that was not a conscious choice on my part. In fact, because my plays had all been explicitly tied to religion—to Christianity in general and Mormonism in particular—when I turned my hand to writing science fiction and fantasy I made a deliberate choice to *exclude* religious concerns from my writing. No one was going to be a member of the Mormon Church; there were going to be no tales of prophets, saviors, priests, or believers. I was going to write pure, unmixed sci-fi.

This was not because of any hostility toward religion, you understand. I have been a believing and practicing Latter-day Saint throughout my writing career, without wavering on that point. I am, in fact, quite annoyed with critics who assume that this or that bit of my writing clearly shows my "struggles with doubt," as if the only religious issue worth writing about was whether or not one believes in a particular religion. That, in fact, is the most elementary—dare I say childish?—religious issue, and the one least interesting to those who are actually committed to a faith. There seems to be an idea among those obsessed with their own unbelief that to write about religion means to write about doubt. They miss the point. To write about religion actually means to write about truth and faith, two matters that cannot be intelligently dealt with in the presence of doubt. They can be dealt with easily in the face of unbelief—it is doubt itself that muddies the waters. You cannot present an idea clearly if you spend all your time discussing whether it's true. You leave the issue of truth in abeyance while you discover what the idea is; only then, having understood, should the issue of doubt vs. belief arise. And, quite frankly, I'm just as happy if it arises after the story is over.

This is one of the things that has caused most damage to Mormon fiction—the obsessive concern so many writers have with people coming into or leaving the Church. It's what I call "revolving door fiction," and I'm weary of it. It suggests that the writers themselves are not yet adults in the matter of religion, not yet committed to a path. I don't despise their personal struggle, but I do wish they'd find something else to write about.

Because what's really interesting about religious people is what happens *after* the commitment is made, and that is precisely what can't be written about by people who have never made one.

My impatience with badly conceived Mormon fiction (and drama, for that matter) was part of my reason for eschewing overtly religious topics or characters in my science fiction. To my surprise, however, I discovered that my work had become more, not less, religious when I stopped dealing with religious subjects consciously. I would go to a convention and somebody would ask me, "Are you Mormon?" "Yes," I'd say. "Oh, I knew it before I was halfway through reading *A Planet Called Treason* [or *Songmaster* or *Hot Sleep*]." Horrified, I would demand to know what it was that made my work seem so obviously Mormon. When they pointed it out, it would be just as obvious to me—but until that moment I had been completely unaware of it. It seemed that I was writing religious fiction whether I wanted to or not.

But those unconsciously religious elements were exactly the kind of religious writing I was talking about before—explorations of the relationship between human beings and the purposer or purposers of life. There was another kind of writing about religion that I gradually began to want to write. I wanted to write, not only about religious ideas, but also about religious *people.* Yet I wanted to do it without writing "inspirational literature"—the kind of stuff that gets published in the Religious Fiction category.

Rare indeed is the human society that does not have a powerful religious ritual binding it together. Pluralism such as we have in America is extremely rare, and I think it's fair to say that it exists even in America only as the result of a conscious effort that is not always happily received by the American people. The very pervasiveness of Christmas and the deep resentment felt by many—perhaps most—Americans about the seemingly absurd finickiness of the courts in their effort to keep government bodies from promoting Christian Christmas rituals show that pluralism does not come easily or naturally even to a people with a two-century history of commitment to it.

Yet if you read most science fiction you wouldn't have a clue that religion played a part in anyone's life. Most sci-fi characters are utterly untouched by religion, by ritual, or by faith, *except* when religious rituals or faith are used to show how benighted or depraved or primitive a particular group or individual is. This is actually right in line with contemporary American literary fiction, so it isn't just because of a pro-science bias on the part of the writers. Yet this is so contrary to reality and betrays such a profound ignorance on the part of the writers that it should betray to most people a rather uncomfortable fact: American writers tend not to be in tune with America. Or, to put it another way, religious Americans and literary Americans have, consciously or not, separated themselves almost completely.

I think what happens is that religious people

who are becoming writers get the idea, from their reading and from the public attitudes of most fashionable writers, that it's faintly embarrassing to present religion as a matter-of-fact part of life, rather like wearing colors that clash. Writers who would vigorously resist any attempt at censorship, or even editorial pressure to change an idea or a word or a comma, rigorously remove from their work—in fact, don't even allow themselves to conceive of putting it into their work in the first place—anything that might suggest that they harbor some sympathy for a particular religion or faith.

Even those who do deal with religious people positively take great care to distance themselves from it. Garrison Keillor, for example, keeps quite a common distance between himself and the Catholics and Lutherans of Lake Woebegon; he likes them, but he isn't *one* of them. Indeed, this sort of attitude may well arise from many authors' experience, for most religious communities don't react well to strangeness, and the kind of character traits that lead one to be a storyteller are generally classed as strange. Much of the avoidance of or hostility to religious people in American fiction may arise out of writers' painful experiences with religion in their growing-up years.

But the current American trend of almost absolute hostility toward or neglect of characters who have a religious life goes beyond anything that could be accounted for in individual lives. If people's real experiences with religion were so universally hideous, religions could not survive. I know from experience that religious people are as likely to be bright, good-hearted, and open-minded as nonreligious people. I have found proportionately as many bigots, cretins, and would-be fascists among university intellectuals as I have among practitioners of any religion I've known at all well. I've also found that religious people tend to have a much better knowledge and clearer understanding of unreligious people than the latter have of the former. The ignorance is mutual, but the nonreligious people have a bit more than their share.

So in this last decade I have turned more and more toward trying to give my characters a religious life, and to undo the skewed picture of religion that is almost completely universal in contemporary American letters. That there are abuses to be satirized cannot be doubted, and I do my share, in stories like "Saving Grace" and "Eye for Eye." But there are also graceful elements in the life of religious communities, and good people whose religion is part of their expression of their goodness, and such things also ought to be shown.

I deal with this most explicitly in my novel *Speaker for the Dead*, where I have the story's hero and title character, Andrew Wiggin, come to a small colony in which Brazilian Catholicism is the established church. I deliberately began the relationship between Wiggin and the Catholics by having the bishop of Lusitania warn his people against the speaker for the dead; and Andrew quickly runs into great resistance from the people because of the bishop's hostility. In short, I began with the cliché relationship between Wiggin the humanist and a religious community.

Then I set out to transform that relationship—and, with luck, the attitude of the reader. First, I introduced some positive religious characters—a husband and wife from a teaching order called the Children of the Mind of Christ. They were tolerant of, even cooperative with, the speaker for the dead, and they were also the guardians of scientific knowledge and liberal education in Lusitania. Yet they were also absolutely committed to a monastic law that required them to marry but forbade them to have sex, and I labored to make this painful religious sacrifice seem, not bizarre, but beautiful to the reader. It is not something I would personally ever want to do, nor do I advocate it; but I wanted readers to realize that such a painful choice, made for the sake of religion, did not debase the characters but rather ennobled them.

Second, I carefully transformed the readers' understanding of the bishop himself. As the novel progresses, we begin to see that his hostility to Wiggin was not entirely because of closed-mindedness, but primarily because of a real concern for the welfare of his people. And as his perception of the needs of the people changed, we saw that the bishop—like all good religious leaders—was willing to do what was necessary for his people, even if it meant temporarily allying himself with a humanist minister like the speaker for the dead.

Finally, I showed that Andrew Wiggin himself, as he gradually comes to be part of one family and part of the community at large, realizes that to really belong he must also be a Catholic. He had been baptized a Catholic in his infancy—something that I had put into *Ender's Game* just for fun, but now found quite useful—and so as part of joining Novinha's family and Lusitania itself, he begins to attend mass and act out the rituals of the church. The issue of faith doesn't arise. What matters is belonging to the community and subjecting himself to the community's most basic discipline.

This is not to say that I show religion in a completely favorable light. The struggle with sin is what nearly destroys Novinha and her family. The people are every bit as intolerant of strangeness as any small town, and their intolerance is embedded within their religious life. They are also superstitious and try to use religion like magic. But in *Speaker for the Dead* I try to put these things in perspective. They are part of religious life, but not all of it; and religion brings at least as much goodness and comfort as it brings pain into the characters' lives.

My point was not to show that religion is all good—it isn't. My point was, first, to recognize what most writers seem to ignore, that most people throughout the world and throughout history are believing members of a religious community—and that usually their religion and their citizenship are indistinguishable. Then, second, I was determined to undermine the fashionably hostile stereotypes that mark American fiction whenever it *does* include religion. *Speaker for the Dead* is not a religious book, at least not in the sense that a religious book might demand that you decide whether you believe or don't believe, belong or don't belong. But it does include religion in its realistic and proper proportion in human life. In that sense it is far more realistic than most American novels.

Over the years religion has cropped up more and more in my work, until finally, with a series of short stories that became the book *The Folk of the Fringe*, I dealt explicitly with Mormon characters and Mormon culture in a near-future setting. Oddly enough, these stories—which, because of their separate existence in that book, do not appear in this collection—are actually some of the *least* religious of my writing, in that they are *not* about the relationship between the living and the purpose of life. Rather they are almost anthropological in their treatment of Mormonism. They are about the way people connect with and abrade against each other within the tight confines of a demanding religious community.

So I write three kinds of fiction that deals with religion. First, like many, perhaps most, science fiction writers, I tell stories that deal with the purpose of life—with the relationship between man and God. Second, I tell stories that deliberately subvert the clichés about religion that are so widespread in American fiction, by showing religious characters in a full range of roles within my stories. And, third, I tell stories that include my direct experience of religious life by depicting the community I know best, Mormonism.

At no point am I trying to persuade you; I want readers, not proselytes. With *Cruel Miracles* I have drawn together my stories that most clearly deal with religious matters not often touched upon by contemporary American writers, matters like holiness, awe, faith, comfort, responsibility, and community. You don't have to be a religious person or even *like* religious people to receive these stories. I hope, though, that by the end you understand a little more about the religious aspect of human life.

MORTAL GODS

T HE FIRST CONTACT was peaceful, almost uneventful: sudden landings near government
buildings all over the world, brief discussions in
the native languages, followed by treaties allowing
the aliens to build certain buildings in certain
places in exchange for certain favors—nothing
spectacular. The technological improvements
that the aliens brought helped make life better for
everyone, but they were improvements that were
already well within the reach of human engineers
within the next decade or two. And the greatest
gift of all was found to be a disappointment—
space travel. The aliens did not have faster-than-
light travel. Instead, they had conclusive proof
that faster-than-light travel was utterly impossible. They had infinite patience and incredibly long

lives to sustain them in their snail's-pace crawl among the stars, but humans would be dead before even the shortest space flight was fairly begun.

And after only a little while, the presence of aliens was regarded as quite the normal thing. They insisted that they had no further gifts to bring, and simply exercised their treaty rights to build and visit the buildings they had made.

The buildings were all different from each other, but had one thing in common: by the standards of the local populace, the new alien buildings were all clearly recognizable as churches.

Mosques. Cathedrals. Shrines. Synagogues. Temples. All unmistakably churches.

But no congregation was invited, though any person who came to such a place was welcomed by whatever aliens happened to be there at the time, who engaged in charming discussion totally related to the person's own interests. Farmers conversed about farming, engineers about engineering, housewives about motherhood, dreamers about dreams, travelers about travels, astronomers about the stars. Those who came and talked went away feeling good. Feeling that someone did, indeed, attach importance to their lives—had come trillions of kilometers through incredible boredom (five hundred years in space, they said!) just to see *them*.

And gradually life settled into a peaceful routine. Scientists, it is true, kept on discovering, and engineers kept on building according to those discoveries, and so changes *did* come. But knowing now that there was no great scientific revolution just around the corner, no tremendous discovery that would open up the stars, men and women settled down, by and large, to the business of being happy.

It wasn't as hard as people had supposed.

Willard Crane was an old man, but a content one. His wife was dead, but he did not resent the brief interregnum in his life in which he was solitary again, a thing he had not been since he came home from the Vietnam War with half a foot missing and found his girl waiting for him anyway, foot or no foot. They had lived all their married lives in a house in the Avenues of Salt Lake City, which, when they moved there, had been a shabby, dilapidated relic of a previous century, but which now was a splendid preservation of a noble era in architecture. Willard was in that comfortable area between heavy wealth and heavier poverty; enough money to satisfy normal aspirations, but not enough money to tempt him to extravagance.

Every day he walked from 7th Avenue and L Street to the cemetery, not far away, where practically everyone had been buried. It was there, in the middle of the cemetery, that the alien building stood—an obvious mimic of old Mormon temple architecture, meaning it was a monstrosity of conflicting periods that somehow, perhaps through intense sincerity, managed to be beautiful anyway.

And there he sat among the gravestones, watching as occasional people wandered into and out of the sanctuary where the aliens came, visited, left.

Happiness is boring as hell, he decided one day. And so, to provoke a little delightful variety, he decided to pick a fight with somebody. Unfortunately, everyone he knew at all well was too nice to fight. And so he decided that he had a bone to pick with the aliens.

When you're old, you can get away with anything.

He went to the alien temple and walked inside.

On the walls were murals, paintings, maps; on the floor, pedestals with statues; it seemed more a museum than anything else. There were few places to sit, and he saw no sign of aliens. Which wouldn't be a disaster; just deciding on a good argument had been variety enough, noting with pride the fine quality of the work the aliens had chosen to display.

But there was an alien there, after all.

"Good morning, Mr. Crane," said the alien.

"How the hell you know my name?"

"You perch on a tombstone every morning and watch as people come in and go out. We found you fascinating. We asked around." The alien's voicebox was very well programmed—a warm, friendly, interested voice. And Willard was too old and jaded with novelty to get much excited about the way the alien slithered along the floor and slopped on the bench next to him like a large, self-moving piece of seaweed.

"We wished you would come in."

"I'm in."

"And why?"

Now that the question was put, his reason

seemed trivial to him; but he decided to play the game all the way through. Why not, after all? "I have a bone to pick with you."

"Heavens," said the alien, with mock horror.

"I have some questions that have never been answered to my satisfaction."

"Then I trust we'll have some answers."

"All right then." But what *were* his questions? "You'll have to forgive me if my mind gets screwed around. The brain dies first, as you know."

"We know."

"Why'd you build a temple here? How come you build churches?"

"Why, Mr. Crane, we've answered that a thousand times. We *like* churches. We find them the most graceful and beautiful of all human architecture."

"I don't believe you," Willard said. "You're dodging my question. So let me put it another way. How come you have the time to sit around and talk to half-assed imbeciles like me? Haven't you got anything better to do?"

"Human beings are unusually good company. It's a most pleasant way to pass the time which does, after many years, weigh rather heavily on our, um, hands." And the alien tried to gesture with his pseudopodia, which was amusing, and Willard laughed.

"Slippery bastards, aren't you?" he inquired, and the alien chuckled. "So let me put it this way, and no dodging, or I'll know you have something to hide. You're pretty much like us, right? You have the same gadgets, but you can travel in space because you don't croak after a hundred years like we do; whatever, you do pretty much the same kinds of things we do. And yet—"

"There's always an 'and yet,' " the alien sighed.

"And *yet*. You come all the way out here, which ain't exactly Main Street, Milky Way, and all you do is build these churches all over the place and sit around and jaw with whoever the hell comes in. Makes no sense, sir, none at all."

The alien oozed gently toward him. "Can you keep a secret?"

"My old lady thought she was the only woman I ever slept with in my life. Some secrets I can keep."

"Then here is one to keep. We come, Mr. Crane, to worship."

"Worship who?"

"Worship, among others, you."

Willard laughed long and loud, but the alien looked (as only aliens can) terribly earnest and sincere.

"Listen, you mean to tell me that you worship *people*?"

"Oh, yes. It is the dream of everyone who dares to dream on my home planet to come here and meet a human being or two and then live on the memory forever."

And suddenly it wasn't funny to Willard anymore. He looked around—human art in prominent display, the whole format, the choice of churches. "You aren't joking."

"No, Mr. Crane. We've wandered the galaxy

for several million years, all told, meeting new races and renewing acquaintance with old. Evolution is a tedious old highway—carbon-based life always leads to certain patterns and certain forms, despite the fact that we seem hideously different to you—"

"Not too bad, Mister, a little ugly, but not too bad—"

"All the—people like us that you've seen—well, we don't come from the same planet, though it has been assumed so by your scientists. Actually, we come from thousands of planets. Separate, independent evolution, leading inexorably to us. Absolutely, or nearly absolutely, uniform throughout the galaxy. We are the natural endproduct of evolution."

"So we're the oddballs."

"You might say so. Because somewhere along the line, Mr. Crane, deep in your past, your planet's evolution went astray from the normal. It created something utterly new."

"Sex?"

"We all have sex, Mr. Crane. Without it, how in the world could the race improve? No, what was new on your planet, Mr. Crane, was death."

The word was not an easy one for Willard to hear. His wife had, after all, meant a great deal to him. And he meant even more to himself. Death already loomed in dizzy spells and shortened breath and weariness that refused to turn into sleep.

"Death?"

"We don't die, Mr. Crane. We reproduce by

splitting off whole sections of ourselves with identical DNA—you know about DNA?"

"I went to college."

"And with us, of course, as with all other life in the universe, intelligence is carried on the DNA, not in the brain. One of the byproducts of death, the brain is. We don't have it. We split, and the individual, complete with all memories, lives on in the children, who are made up of the actual flesh of my flesh, you see? I will never die."

"Well, bully for you," Willard said, feeling strangely cheated, and wondering why he hadn't guessed.

"And so we came here and found people whose life had a finish; who began as unformed creatures without memory and, after an incredibly brief span, died."

"And for that you worship us? I might as well go worshiping bugs that die a few minutes after they're born."

The alien chuckled, and Willard resented it.

"Is that why you come here? To gloat?"

"What else would we worship, Mr. Crane? While we don't discount the possibility of invisible gods, we really never have invented any. We never died, so why dream of immortality? Here we found a people who knew how to worship, and for the first time we found awakened in us a desire to do homage to superior beings."

And Willard noticed his heartbeat, realized that it would stop while the alien had no heart, had nothing that would ever end. "Superior, hell."

"We," said the alien, "remember everything,

from the first stirrings of intellect to the present. When we are 'born,' so to speak, we have no need of teachers. We have never learned to write—merely to exchange RNA. We have never learned to create beauty to outlast our lives because nothing outlasts our lives. We live to see all our works crumble. Here, Mr. Crane, we have found a race that builds for the sheer joy of building, that creates beauty, that writes books, that invents the lives of never-known people to delight others who know they are being lied to, a race that devises immortal gods to worship and celebrates its own mortality with immense pomp and glory. Death is the foundation of all that is great about humanity, Mr. Crane."

"Like hell it is," said Willard. "I'm about to die, and there's nothing great about it."

"You don't really believe that, Mr. Crane," the alien said. "None of you do. Your lives are built around death, glorifying it. Postponing it as long as possible, to be sure, but glorifying it. In the earliest literature, the death of the hero is the moment of greatest climax. The most potent myth."

"Those poems weren't written by old men with flabby bodies and hearts that only beat when they feel like it."

"Nonsense. Everything you do smacks of death. Your poems have beginnings and endings, and structures that limit the work. Your paintings have edges, marking off where the beauty begins and ends. Your sculptures isolate a moment in time. Your music starts and finishes. All that you do is mortal—it is all born. It all dies. And yet you struggle against mortality and have overcome it, building up tremendous stores of shared knowledge through your finite books and your finite words. You put frames on everything."

"Mass insanity, then. But it explains nothing about why you worship. You must come here to mock us."

"Not to mock you. To envy you."

"Then die. I assume that your protoplasm or whatever is vulnerable."

"You don't understand. A human being can die—*after* he has reproduced—and all that he knew and all that he has will live on after him. But if *I* die, I cannot reproduce. My knowledge dies with me. An awesome responsibility. We cannot assume it. I *am* all the paintings and writings and songs of a million generations. To die would be the death of a civilization. You have cast yourselves free of life and achieved greatness."

"And that's why you come here."

"If ever there were gods. If ever there was power in the universe. You are those gods. You have that power."

"We have no power."

"Mr. Crane, you are beautiful."

And the old man shook his head, stood with difficulty, and doddered out of the temple and walked away slowly among the graves.

"You tell them the truth," said the alien to no one in particular (to future generations of himself who would need the memory of the words having been spoken), "and it only makes it worse."

* * *

It was only seven months later, and the weather was no longer spring, but now blustered with the icy wind of late autumn. The trees in the cemetery were no longer colorful; they were stripped of all but the last few brown leaves. And into the cemetery walked Willard Crane again, his arms half enclosed by the metal crutches that gave him, in his old age, four points of balance instead of the precarious two that had served him for more than ninety years. A few snowflakes were drifting lazily down, except when the wind snatched them and spun them in crazy dances that had neither rhythm nor direction.

Willard laboriously climbed the steps of the temple.

Inside, an alien was waiting.

"I'm Willard Crane," the old man said.

"And I'm an alien. You spoke to me—or my parent, however you wish to phrase it—several months ago."

"Yes."

"We knew you'd come back."

"Did you? I vowed I never would."

"But we know you. You are well known to us all, Mr. Crane. There are billions of gods on Earth for us to worship, but you are the noblest of them all."

"I am?"

"Because only you have thought to do us the kindest gift. Only you are willing to let us watch your death."

And a tear leaped from the old man's eye as he blinked heavily.

"Is that why I came?"

"Isn't it?"

"I thought I came to damn your souls to hell, that's why I came, you bastards, coming to taunt me in the final hours of my life."

"You came to us."

"I wanted to show you how ugly death is."

"Please. Do."

And, seemingly eager to oblige them, Willard's heart stopped and he, in brief agony, slumped to the floor in the temple.

The aliens all slithered in, all gathered around closely, watching him rattle for breath.

"I will not die!" he savagely whispered, each breath an agony, his face fierce with the heroism of struggle.

And then his body shuddered and he was still.

The aliens knelt there for hours in silent worship as the body became cold. And then, at last, because they had learned this from their gods— that words must be said to be remembered—one of them spoke:

"Beautiful," he said tenderly. "Oh Lord my God," he said worshipfully.

And they were gnawed within by the grief of knowing that this greatest gift of all gifts was forever out of their reach.

SAVING GRACE

And he looked into her eyes, and lo!
when her gaze fell upon him
he did verily turn to stone,
for her visage was wondrous ugly.
Praise the Lord.

MOTHER CAME HOME depressed as hell with a bag full of groceries and a headache fit to make her hair turn to snakes. Billy, he knew when Mommy was like that, he could tell as soon as she grumped through the living room. But if she was full of hellfire, he had the light of heaven, and so he said, "Don't be sad, Mother, Jesus loves you."

Mother put the margarine into the fridge and

wiped the graham cracker crumbs off the table and dumped them in the sink even though the disposal hadn't worked for years. "Billy," she said quietly, "you been saved again?"

"I only was just going to look inside."

"Ought to sue those bastards. Burn down their tent or something. Why can't they do their show from a studio like everybody else?"

"I felt my sins just weighing me down and then he reached out and Jesus come into my heart and I had to be baptized."

At the word *baptized*, Mommy slammed the kitchen counter. The mixing bowl bounced. "*Not* again, you damn near got pneumonia the last time!"

"This time I dried my hair."

"It isn't sanitary!"

"I was the first one in. Everybody was crying."

"Well, you just listen! I tell you not to go there, and I mean it! You look at me when I'm talking to you, young man."

Her irresistible fingers lifted up his chin. Billy felt like he was living in a Bible story. He could almost hear Bucky Fay himself telling the tale: And he looked into her eyes, and lo! when her gaze fell upon him he did verily turn to stone, and he could not move though he sorely feared that he might wet his pants, for her visage was wondrous ugly. Praise the Lord.

"Now you promise me you won't go into that tent anymore, ever, because you got no resistance at all, you just come straight home, you hear me?"

He could not move until at last she despaired and looked away, and then he found his voice and said, "What *else* am I supposed to do after school?"

Today was different from all the other times they had this argument: this time his mother leaned on the counter and sobbed into the waffle mix. Billy came and put his arm around her and leaned his head on her hip. She turned and held him close and said, "If that son-of-a-bitch hadn't left me you might've had some brothers and sisters to come home to." They made waffles together, and while Billy pried pieces of overcooked waffle out of the waffle iron with a bent table knife, he vowed that he would not cause his mother such distress again. The revival tent could flap its wings and lift up its microwave dish to take part in the largess of heaven, but Billy would look the other way for his mother's sake, for she had suffered enough.

Yet he couldn't keep his thoughts away from the tent, because when they were telling what was coming up soon they had said that Bucky Fay was coming. Bucky Fay, the healer of channel 49, who had been known to exorcise that demon cancer and cast out kidney stones in the name of the Lord; Bucky Fay, who looked to Billy like the picture Mommy kept hidden in the back of her top drawer, the picture of his father, the son-of-a-bitch. Billy wanted to see the man with the healing hands, see him in the flesh.

"Mommy," he said. On TV the skinny people were praising Diet Pepsi.

"Mm?" Mommy didn't look up.

"I wish my foot was all twisted up so I couldn't walk."

Now she looked up. "My Lord, what for!"

"So Jesus could turn it around."

"Billy, that's disgusting."

"When the miracle goes through you, Mommy, it knocks you on the head and then you fall down and get all better. A little girl with no arm got a new arm from God. They said so."

"Child, they've turned you superstitious."

"I wish I had a club foot, so Jesus would do a miracle on me."

God moves in mysterious ways, but this time he was pretty direct. Of all the half-assed wishes that got made and prayers that got said, Billy's got answered. Billy's mother was brooding about how the boy was going off the deep end. She decided she had to get him out doing things that normal kids do. The movie playing at the local family-oriented moviehouse was the latest go-round of *Pollyanna*. They went and watched and Billy learned a lesson. Billy saw how *good* this little girl was, and how preachers liked her, and first thing you know he was up on the roof, figuring out how to fall off just right so you smash your legs but don't break your back.

Never did get it right. Broke his back, clean as could be, spinal cord severed just below the shoulders, and there he was in a wheelchair, wearing diapers and pissing into a plastic bag. In the hospital he watched TV, a religious station that had God's chosen servants on all day, praising and

praying and saving. And they had Bucky Fay himself, praise the Lord, Bucky Fay himself making
the deaf to hear and the arthritic to move around
and the audience to be generous, and there sat
Billy, more excited than he had ever been before,
because now he was ripe and ready for a miracle.

"Not a chance in the world," his mother said.
"By God I'm going to get you uncrazy, and the last
place I'm going to take you is anywhere in earshot
of those lying cheating hypocritical so-called healers."

But there's not many people in the world can
say no more than two or three times to a paralyzed
kid in a wheelchair, especially if he's crying, and
besides, Mommy thought, maybe there's something *to* faith. Lord knows the boy's got *that*, even
if he doesn't have a single nerve in his legs. And
if there's even a chance of maybe giving him back
some of his body, what harm can it do?

Once inside the tent, of course, she thought of
other things. What if it *is* a fraud, which of course
it is, and what happens when the boy finds out?
What then? So she whispered to him, "Billy, now
don't go expecting too much."

"I'm not." Just a miracle, that's all. They do
them all the time, Mommy.

"I just don't want you to be disappointed when
nothing happens."

"I won't be disappointed, Mommy." No. He'll
fix me right up.

And then the nice lady leaned over and asked,
"You here to be healed?"

Billy only nodded, recognizing her as Bucky

Fay's helper lady who always said "Oh, my sweet Lord Jesus you're so kind" when people got healed, said it in a way that made your spine tingle. She was wearing a lot of makeup. Billy could see she had a moustache with makeup really packed onto it. He wondered if she was really secretly a man as she wheeled him up to the front. But why would a man wear a dress? He was wondering about that as she got him in place, lined up with the other wheelchair people on the front row.

A man came along and knelt down in front of him. Billy got ready to pray, but the man just talked normal, so Billy opened his eyes. "Now this one's going on TV," the man said, "and for the TV show we need you to be real careful, son. Don't say anything unless Bucky asks you a direct question, and then you just tell him real quick. Like when he asks you how come you got in a wheelchair, what'll you tell him?"

"I'll say—I'll say—"

"Now don't go freezing up on him, or it'll look real bad. This is on TV, remember. Now you just tell me how come you got in a wheelchair."

"So I could get healed by the power of Jesus."

The man looked at him a moment, and then he said, "Sure. I guess you'll do just fine. Now when it's all over, and you're healed, I'll be right there, holding you by the arm. Now don't say Thank the Lord right off. You wait till I squeeze your arm, and then you say it. Okay?"

"Okay."

"For the TV, you know."

"Yeah."

"Don't be nervous."

"I won't."

The man went away but he was back in just a second looking worried. "You can feel things in your arms, can't you?"

Billy lifted his arms and waved them up and down. "My arms are just fine." The man nodded and went away again.

There was nothing to do but watch, then, and Billy watched, but he didn't see much. On the TV, all you could see was Bucky Fay, but here the camera guys kept getting in front of him, and people were going back and forth all during the praising time and the support this ministry time so Billy could hardly keep track of what was going on. Till the man who talked to him came over to him again, and this time a younger guy was with him, and they lifted Billy out of his chair and carried him over toward where the lights were so bright, and the cameras were turned toward him, and Bucky Fay was saying, "And now who is first, thanks be to the Lord? Are you that righteous young man who the devil has cursed to be a homophiliac? Come here, boy! God's going to give you a blood transfusion from the hemoglobin of the Holy Spirit!"

Billy didn't know what to do. If he said anything before Bucky Fay asked him a question, the man would be mad, but what good would it do if Bucky Fay ordered up the wrong miracle? But then he saw how the man who had talked to him turned his face away from the camera and mouthed, "Paralyzed," and Bucky Fay caught it and went right on, saying "Do you think the Saviour is worried? Paralyzed you are, too, completely helpless, and yet when the miracle comes into your body, do you think the Holy Spirit needs the doctor's diagnosis? No, praise the Lord, the Holy Spirit goes all through you, hunting down every place where the devil has hurt you, where the devil that great serpent has *poisoned* you, where the devil that mighty dragon has thought he could *destroy* you—boy, are you saved?"

It was a direct question. "Uh huh."

"Has the Lord come to you in the waters of baptism and washed away your sins and made you clean?"

Billy wasn't sure what that all meant, but after a second the man squeezed his arm, and so Billy said, "Thank the Lord."

"What the baptism did to the outside of your body, the miracle will do to the inside of your body. Do you believe that Jesus can heal you?"

Billy nodded.

"Oh, be not ashamed, little child. Speak so all the millions of our television friends can hear you. Can Jesus heal you?"

"Yes! I know he can!"

Bucky Fay smiled, and his face went holy; he spat on his hands, clapped twice, and then slapped Billy in the forehead, splashing spit all over his face. Just that very second the two men holding him sort of half-dropped him, and as he clutched forward with his hands he realized that all those times when people seemed to be overcome by the Holy Spirit, they were just getting *dropped*, but that was probably part of the miracle. They got him down on the floor and Bucky Fay went on talking about the Lord knowing the pure in heart, and then the two men picked him up and this time stood him on his legs. Billy couldn't feel a thing, but he did know that he was standing. They were helping him balance, but his weight was on his legs, and the miracle had worked. He almost praised God right then, but he remembered in time, and waited.

"I bet you feel a little weak, don't you," said Bucky Fay.

Was that a direct question? Billy wasn't sure, so he just nodded his head.

"When the Holy Spirit went through the Apostle Paul, didn't he lie upon the ground? Already you are able to stand upon your legs, and after a good night's sleep, when your body has strengthened itself after being inhabited by the Spirit of the Lord, you'll be restored to your whole self, good as new!"

Then the man squeezed Billy's arm. "Praise the Lord," Billy said. But that was wrong—it was supposed to be thank the Lord, and so he said it even louder, "Thank the Lord."

And now with the cameras on him, the two men holding him worked the real miracle, for they turned him and leaned him forward, and pulled him along back to the wheelchair. As they pulled him, they rocked him back and forth, and under him Billy could hear his shoes scuffing the ground, left, right, left, right, just as if he was walking. But he wasn't walking. He couldn't feel a thing. And then he knew. All those miracles, all those walking people—they had men beside them, leaning them left, leaning them right, making their legs fall forward, just like dolls, just like dummies, real dummies. And Billy cried. They got the camera real close to him then, to show the tears streaking down his face. The crowd applauded and praised.

"He's new at walking," Bucky Fay shouted into the microphone. "He isn't used to so much exercise. Let that boy ride in his chair again until he has a chance to build up his strength. But praise the Lord! We know that the miracle is done, Jesus has given this boy his legs and healed his hemophobia, too!" As the woman wheeled him down the aisle, the people reached out to touch him, said kind and happy things to him, and he cried. His mother was crying for joy. She embraced him and said, "You walked," and Billy cried harder. Out in the car he told her the truth. She looked off toward the brightly lit door of that flamboyant, that seductive tent, and she said, "God damn him to burn in hell forever." But Billy was quite, quite sure that God would do no such thing.

Not that Billy doubted God. No, God had all power, God was a granter of prayers. God was even fair-minded, after his fashion. But Billy knew now that when God set himself to balance things in the world, he did it sneaky. He did it tricky. He did it ass-backward, so that anybody who wanted to could see his works in the world and still doubt God. After all, what good was faith if God went around leaving plain evidence of his goodness in the world? No, not God. His goodness would be kept a profound secret, Billy knew that. Just a secret God kept to himself.

And sure enough, when God set out to even things up for Billy, he didn't do the obvious thing. He didn't let the nerves heal, he didn't send the miracle of feeling, the blessing of pain into Billy's empty legs. Instead God, who probably had a bet on with Satan about this one, gave Billy another gift entirely, an unlooked-for blessing that would break his heart.

Mother was wheeling Billy around the park. It was a fine summer day, which means that the humidity was so high that fish could live for days out of the water. Billy was dripping sweat, and he knew that when he got home he'd have a hell of a diaper rash, and Mother would say, "Oh you poor dear," and Billy would grieve because it didn't even itch. The river was flowing low and there were big rocks uncovered by the shore. Billy sat there watching the kids climb around on the rocks. His mother saw what he was watching and tried to take him away so he wouldn't get depressed about how he couldn't climb, but Billy wouldn't let her. He just stayed and watched. He picked out one kid in particular, a pretty-faced body with a muscled chest, about two years older than Billy. He watched everything that boy did, and pretended that he was doing it. That was a good thing to do, Billy would rather do that than anything, watch this boy play for him on the rocks.

But all the time there was this idiot girl watching *Billy*. She was on the grass, far back from the shore, where all the cripples have to stay. She walked like an inchworm almost, each step a major event, as if she was a big doll with a little driver inside working the controls, and the driver wasn't very good at it yet. Billy tried to watch the golden body of the pretty-faced boy, but this spastic girl kept lurching around at the edges of his eyes.

"Make that retard go away," Billy whispered.

"What?" asked Mother.

"I don't want to look at that retard girl."

"Then don't look at her."

"Make her go away. She keeps looking at me."

Mother patted Billy's shoulder. "Other people got rights, Billy. I can't make her go away from the park. You want me to take you somewhere else?"

"No." Not while the golden boy was standing tall on the rocks, extending himself to snatch Frisbies out of the air without falling. Like God catching lightning and laughing in delight.

The spastic girl came closer and closer, in her sidewise way. And Billy grew more and more determined not to pay the slightest heed to her. It was obvious, though, that she was coming to him, that she meant to reach him, and as he sat there he grew afraid. What would she do? His greatest fear was of someone snatching his urine bag from between his legs and holding it up, the catheter tugging away at him, and everybody laughing and laughing. That was what he hated worst, living his life like a tire with a slow leak. He knew that she would grab between his legs for the urine bag under his lap robe, and probably spill it all over, she was such a spastic. But he said nothing of his fear, just waited, holding onto his lap robe, watching the golden boy jump from the highest rock into the river in order to splash the kids who were perched on the lesser rocks.

Then the spastic girl touched him. Thumped her club of a hand into his arm and moaned loudly. Billy cried out, "Oh, God!" The girl shuddered and fell to the ground, weeping.

All at once every single person in the park ran over and leaned around, jostling and looking. Billy held tight to his lap robe, lest someone pull it away. The spastic girl's parents were all apology, she'd never done anything like that, she usually just kept to herself, we're so sorry, so *terribly* sorry. They lifted the girl to her feet, tried to lead her away, but she shrugged them off violently. She shuddered again, and formed her mouth elaborately to make a word. Her parents watched her lips intently, but when the words came, they were clear. "I am better," she said.

Carefully she took a step, not toward her parents, but toward Billy. The step was not a lurch controlled by a clumsy little puppeteer. It was slow and uncertain, but it was a human step. "He healed me," she said.

Step after step, each more deft than the last, and Billy forgot all about his lap robe. She was healed, she was whole. She had touched him and now she was cured.

"Praise God," someone in the crowd said.

"It's just like on TV," someone else said.

"Saw it with my own two eyes."

And the girl fell to her knees beside Billy and kissed his hand and wept and wept.

They started coming after that, as word spread. Just a shy-looking man at the front door, a pesky fat lady with a skinny brother, a mother with two mongoloid children. All the freaks in Billy's town, all the sufferers, all the desperate seemed to find the way to his house. "No," Billy told Mother again and again. "I don't want to see nobody."

"But it's a little baby," Mother said. "He's so sweet. He's been through so much pain."

They came in, one by one, and demanded or begged or prayed or just timidly whispered to him, "Heal me." Then Billy would sit there, trembling, as they reached out and touched him. When they knew that they were healed, and they always were, they cried and kissed and praised and thanked and offered money. Billy always refused the money and said precious little else. "Aren't you going to give the glory to God?" asked one lady, whose son Billy healed of leukemia. But Billy just looked at his lap robe until she went away.

The first reporters came from the grocery store papers, the ones that always know about the UFOs. They kept asking him to prophesy the future, until Billy told Mother not to let them come in anymore. Mother tried to keep them out, but they even pretended to be cripples in order to get past the door. They wrote stories about the "crippled healer" and kept quoting Billy as saying things that he never said. They also published his address.

Hundreds of people came every day now, a constant stream all day. One lady with a gimp leg said, "Praise the Lord, it was worth the hundred dollars."

"What hundred dollars?" asked Billy.

"The hundred dollars I give your mother. I give the doctors a thousand bucks and the government give them ten thousand more and they never done a damn thing for me."

Billy called Mother. She came in. "This woman says she gave you a hundred dollars."

"I didn't ask for the money," Mother said.

"Give it back," Billy said.

Mother took the money out of her apron and gave it back. The woman clucked about how she didn't mind either way and left.

"I ain't no Bucky Fay," Billy said.

"Of course you ain't," Mother said. "When people touch you, they get better."

"No money, from nobody."

"That's real smart," Mother said. "I lost my job last week, Billy. I'm home all day just keeping them away from you. How are we going to live?"

Billy just sat there, trying to think about it. "Don't let them in anymore," he said. "Lock the doors and go to work."

Mother started to cry. "Billy, I can't stand it if you don't let them in. All those babies; all those twisted-up people, all those cancers and the fear of death in their faces, I can't stand it except that somehow, by some miracle, when they come in your room and touch you, they come out whole.

I don't know how to turn them away. Jesus gave you a gift I didn't think existed in the world, but it didn't belong to you, Billy. It belongs to *them*."

"I touch myself every day," Billy whispered, "and I never get better."

From then on Mother only took half of whatever people offered, and only *after* they were healed, so people wouldn't get the idea that the healing depended on the money. That way she was able to scrape up enough to keep the roof over their heads and food on the table. "There's a lot less thankful money than bribe money in the world," she said to Billy. Billy just ate, being careful not to spill hot soup on his lap, because he'd never know if he scalded himself.

Then one day the TV cameras came, and the movie cameras, and set up on the lawn and in the street outside.

"What the hell are you doing?" demanded Billy's mother.

"Bucky Fay's coming to meet the crippled healer," said the movie man. "We want to have this for Bucky Fay's show."

"If you try to bring one little camera inside our house I'll have the police on you."

"The public's got a right to know," said the man, pointing the camera at her.

"The public's got a right to kiss my ass," said Mother, and she went back into the house and told everybody to go away and come back tomorrow, they were locking up the house for the day.

Mother and Billy watched through the lacy curtains while Bucky Fay got out of his limousine and waved at the cameras and the people crowded around in the street.

"Don't let him in, Mother," said Billy.

Bucky Fay knocked on the door.

"Don't answer," said Billy.

Bucky Fay knocked and knocked. Then he gestured to the cameramen and they all went back to their vans and all of Bucky Fay's helpers went back to their cars and the police held the crowd far away, and Bucky Fay started talking.

"Billy," said Bucky Fay, "I don't aim to hurt you. You're a true healer, I just want to shake your hand."

"Don't let him touch me again," said Billy. Mother shook her head.

"If you let me help you, you can heal hundreds and hundreds more people, all around the world, and bring millions of TV viewers to Jesus."

"The boy don't want you," Mother said.

"Why are you afraid of me? I didn't give you your gift, God did."

"Go away!" Billy shouted.

There was silence for a moment outside the door. Then Bucky Fay's voice came again, softer, and it sounded like he was holding back a sob. "Billy, why do you think I come to you? I am the worst son-of-a-bitch I know, and I come for you to heal me."

That was not a thing that Billy had ever thought to hear from Bucky Fay.

Bucky Fay was talking soft now, so it was sometimes hard to understand him. "In the name of Jesus, boy, do you think I woke up one morning and said to myself, 'Bucky Fay, go out and be a healer and you'll get rich'? Think I said that? No sir. I had a gift once. Like yours, I had a gift. I found it one day when I was swimming at the water hole with my big brother Jeddy. Jeddy, he was a show-off, he was always tempting Death to come for him, and that day he dove right down from the highest branch and plunked his head smack in the softest, stickiest mud on the bottom of Pachuckamunkey River. Took fifteen minutes just to get his head loose. They brought him to shore and he was dead, his face all covered with mud. And I screamed and cried out loud, 'God, you ain't got no right!' and then I touched my brother, and smacked him on the head, I said, 'God damn you, Jeddy, you pin-headed jackass, you ain't dead, get up and walk!' And that was when I discovered I had the gift. Because Jeddy reached up and wiped the mud off his eyes and rolled over and puked the black Pachukey water all over grass there. 'Thank you Jesus,' I said. In those days I could lay hands on mules with bent legs and they'd go straight. A baby with measles, and his spots would *go*. I had a good heart then. I healed colored people, and in those days even the doctors wouldn't go so far as *that*. But then they offered me money, and I took it, and they asked me to preach even though I didn't know a damn thing, and so I preached, and pretty soon I found myself in a jet airplane that I owned flying over an airstrip that I owned heading for a TV station that I owned and I said to myself, Bucky Fay, *you* haven't healed a soul in twenty years. A few folks have gotten better because of their own faith, but *you* lost the gift. You threw it away for the sake of money." On the other side of the door Bucky Fay wailed in anguish. "Oh, God in heaven, let me in this door or I will die!"

Billy nodded, tears in his eyes, and Mother opened the door. Bucky Fay was on his knees leaning against the door so he nearly fell into the room. He didn't even stand up to walk over to Billy, just crawled most of the way and then said, "Billy, the light of God is in your eyes. Heal me of my affliction! My disease is love of money! My disease is forgetting the Lord God of heaven! Heal me and let me have my gift back again, and I will never stray, not ever so long as I live!"

Billy reached out his hand. Slow and trembling, Bucky Fay gently took that hand and kissed it, and touched it to the tears hot and wet on his cheeks. "You have given me," he said, "you have given me this day a gift that I never thought to have again. I am whole!" He got up, kissed Billy on both cheeks, then stepped back. "Oh, my child, I will pray for you. With all my heart I will pray that God will remove your paralysis from your legs. For I believe he gave you your paralysis to teach you compassion for the cripple, just as he gave me temptation to teach me compassion for the sinner. God bless you, Billy, Hallelujah!"

"Hallelujah," said Billy softly. He was crying too—couldn't help it, he felt so good. He had longed for vengeance, and instead he had forgiven, and he felt *holy*.

That is, until he realized that the TV cameras had come in right behind Bucky Fay, and were taking a close-up of Billy's tear-stained face, of Mother wringing her hands and weeping. Bucky Fay walked out the door, his clenched fist high above his head, and the crowd outside greeted him with a cheer. "Hallelujah!" shouted Bucky. "Jesus has made me whole!"

It played real well on the religious station. Bucky Fay's repentance—oh, how the crowds in the studio audience gasped at his confession. How the people wept at the moment when Billy reached out his hand. It was a fine show. And at the end, Bucky Fay wept again. "Oh, my friends who have trusted me, you have seen the mighty change in my heart. From now on I will wear the one suit that you see me wearing now. I have forsaken my diamond cuff links and my Lear jet and my golf course in Louisiana. I am so ashamed of what I was before God healed me with the hands of that little crippled boy. I tell all of you—send me no more money! Don't send me a single dime to post office box eight three nine, Christian City, Louisiana 70539. I am not fit to have your money. Contribute your tithes and offerings to worthier men than I. Send me *nothing!*—"

Then he knelt and bowed his head for a moment, and then looked up again, out into the audience, into the cameras, tears flowing down his face. "Unless. Unless you forgive me. Unless you believe that Jesus has changed me before your very eyes."

Mother switched off the TV savagely.

"After seeing all those other people get better,"

Billy whispered, "I thought he might've gotten better, too."

Mother shook her head and looked away. "What he got isn't a disease." Then she bent over the wheelchair and hugged him. "I feel so bad, Billy!"

"I don't feel bad," Billy said. "Jesus cured the blind people and the deaf people and the crippled people and the lepers. But as far as I remember, the Bible don't say he ever cured even one son-of-a-bitch."

She was still hugging him, which he didn't mind even though he near smothered in her bosom. Now she chuckled. It was all right, if Mother chuckled about it. "Guess you're right about that," Mother said. "Even Jesus did no better."

For a while they had a rest, because the people who believed went to Bucky Fay and the doubters figured that Billy was no better. The newspaper and TV people stopped coming around, too, because Billy never put on a show for them and never said anything that people would pay money to read. Then, after a while, the sick people started coming back, just a few a week at first, and then more and more. They were uncertain, skeptical. They hadn't heard of Billy on TV lately, hadn't read about him either, and he lived in such a poor neighborhood, with no signs or anything. More than once a car with out-of-state plates drove back and forth in front of the house before it stopped and someone came in. The ones who came were those who had lost all other hope, who were willing to try anything, even something as unlikely as this. They had heard a rumor, someone had a cousin whose best friend was healed. They always felt like such damn fools visiting this crippled kid, but it was better than sitting home waiting for death.

So they came, more and more of them. Mother had to quit her job again. All day Billy waited in his bedroom for them to come in. They always looked so distant, guarding themselves against another disillusionment. Billy, too, was afraid, waiting for the day when someone would place a baby in his arms and the child would die, the healing power gone out of him. But it didn't happen, day after day it didn't happen, and the people kept coming fearful and departing in joy.

Mother and Billy lived pretty poorly, since they only took money that came from gratitude instead of money meant to buy. But Billy had a decent life, if you don't mind being paralyzed and stuck home all the time, and Mother didn't mind too much either, since there was always the sight of the blind seeing and the crippled walking and those withered-up children coming out whole and strong.

Then one day after quite a few years there came a young woman who wasn't sick. She was healthy and tall and nice-looking, in a kitcheny kind of way. She had rolled-up sleeves and hands that looked like they'd met dishwater before, and she walked right into the house and said, "Make room, I'm moving in."

"Now, girl," said Mother, "we got a small house and no room to put you up. I think you got the wrong idea of what kind of Christian charity we offer here."

"Yes, Ma'am. I know just what you do. Because I am the little girl who touched Billy that day by the riverside and started all your misery."

"Now, girl, you know that didn't start our misery."

"I've never forgotten. I grew up and went through two husbands and had no children and no memory of real love except for what I saw in the face of a crippled boy at the riverside, and I thought, 'He needs me, and I need him.' So here I am, I'm here to help, tell me what to do and step aside."

Her name was Madeleine and she stayed from then on. She wasn't noisy and she wasn't bossy, she just worked her share and got along. It was hard to know for sure why it was so, but with Madeleine there, even with no money and no legs, Billy's life was good. They sang a lot of songs, Mother and Billy and Madeleine, sang and played games and talked about a lot of things, when the visitors gave them time. And only once in all those years did Madeleine ever talk to Billy about religion. And then it was just a question.

"Billy," asked Madeleine, "are you God?"

Billy shook his head. "God ain't no cripple."

EYE FOR EYE

JUST TALK, MICK. **Tell us everything. We'll listen.**
Well to start with I know I was doing terrible things. If you're a halfway decent person, you don't go looking to kill people. Even if you can do it without touching them. Even if you can do it so as nobody even guesses they was murdered, you still got to try not to do it.

Who taught you that?
Nobody. I mean it wasn't in the books in the Baptist Sunday School—they spent all their time telling us not to lie or break the sabbath or drink liquor. Never did mention killing. Near as I can figure, the Lord thought killing was pretty smart sometimes, like when Samson done it with a donkey's jaw. A thousand guys dead, but that was okay cause they was Philistines. And lighting

foxes' tails on fire. Samson was a sicko, but he still got his pages in the Bible.

I figure Jesus was about the only guy got much space in the Bible telling people not to kill. And even then, there's that story about how the Lord struck down a guy and his wife cause they held back on their offerings to the Christian church. Oh, Lord, the TV preachers did go on about that. No, it wasn't cause I got religion that I figured out not to kill people.

You know what I think it was? I think it was Vondel Cone's elbow. At the Baptist Children's Home in Eden, North Carolina, we played basketball all the time. On a bumpy dirt court, but we figured it was part- of the game, never knowing which way the ball would bounce. Those boys in the NBA, they play a sissy game on that flat smooth floor.

We played basketball because there wasn't a lot else to do. Only thing they ever had on TV was the preachers. We got it all cabled in—Falwell from up in Lynchburg, Jim and Tammy from Charlotte, Jimmy Swaggart looking hot, Ernest Ainglee looking carpeted, Billy Graham looking like God's executive vice-president—that was all our TV ever showed, so no wonder we lived on the basketball court all year.

Anyway, Vondel Cone wasn't particularly tall and he wasn't particularly good at shooting and on the court nobody was even halfway good at dribbling. But he had elbows. Other guys, when they hit you it was an accident. But when Vondel's elbow met up with your face, he like to pushed your nose out your ear. You can bet we all learned real quick to give him room. He got to take all the shots and get all the rebounds he wanted.

But we got even. We just didn't count his points. We'd call out the score, and any basket he made it was like it never happened. He'd scream and he'd argue and we'd all stand there and nod and agree so he wouldn't punch us out, and then as soon as the next basket was made, we'd call out the score—still not counting Vondel's points. Drove that boy crazy. He screamed till his eyes bugged out, but nobody ever counted his cheating points.

Vondel died of leukemia at the age of fourteen. You see, I never did like that boy.

But I learned something from him. I learned how unfair it was for somebody to get his way just because he didn't care how much he hurt other people. And when I finally realized that I was just about the most hurtful person in the whole world, I knew then and there that it just wasn't right. I mean, even in the Old Testament, Moses said the punishment should fit the crime. Eye for eye, tooth for tooth. Even Steven, that's what Old Peleg said before I killed him of prostate cancer. It was when Peleg got took to the hospital that I left the Eden Baptist Children's Home. Cause I wasn't Vondel. I *did* care how much I hurt folks.

But that doesn't have nothing to do with anything. I don't know what all you want me to talk about.

Just talk, Mick. Tell us whatever you want.

Well I don't aim to tell you my whole life story.

I mean I didn't really start to figure out anything till I got on that bus in Roanoke, and so I can pretty much start there I guess. I remember being careful not to get annoyed when the lady in front of me didn't have the right change for the bus. And I didn't get angry when the bus driver got all snotty and told the lady to get off. It just wasn't worth killing for. That's what I always tell myself when I get mad. It isn't worth killing for, and it helps me calm myself down. So anyway I reached past her and pushed a dollar bill through the slot.

"This is for both of us," I says.

"I don't make change," says he.

I could've just said "Fine" and left it at that, but he was being such a prick that I had to do something to make him see how ignorant he was. So I put another nickel in the slot and said, "That's thirty-five for me, thirty-five for her, and thirty-five for the next guy gets on without no change."

So maybe I provoked him. I'm sorry for that, but I'm human, too, I figure. Anyway he was mad. "Don't you smart off with me, boy. I don't have to let you ride, fare or no fare."

Well, fact was he did, that's the law, and anyway I was white and my hair was short so his boss would probably do something if I complained. I could have told him what for and shut his mouth up tight. Except that if I did, I would have gotten too mad, and no man deserves to die just for being a prick. So I looked down at the floor and said, "Sorry, sir." I didn't say "Sorry *sir*" or anything snotty like that. I said it all quiet and sincere.

If he just *dropped* it, everything would have

been fine, you know? I was mad, yes, but I'd gotten okay at bottling it in, just kind of holding it tight and then waiting for it to ooze away where it wouldn't hurt nobody. But just as I turned to head back toward a seat, he lurched that bus forward so hard that it flung me down and I only caught myself from hitting the floor by catching the handhold on a seatback and half-smashing the poor lady sitting there.

Some other people said, "Hey!" kind of mad, and I realize now that they was saying it to the driver, cause they was on my side. But at the time I thought they was mad at *me*, and that plus the scare of nearly falling and how mad I already was, well, I lost control of myself. I could just feel it in me, like sparklers in my blood veins, spinning around my whole body and then throwing off this pulse that went and hit that bus driver. He was behind me, so I didn't see it with my eyes. But I could feel that sparkiness connect up with him, and twist him around inside, and then finally it came loose from me, I didn't feel it no more. I wasn't mad no more. But I knew I'd done him already.

I even knew where. It was in his liver. I was a real expert on cancer by now. Hadn't I seen everybody I ever knew die of it? Hadn't I read every book in the Eden Public Library on cancer? You can live without kidneys, you can cut out a lung, you can take out a colon and live with a bag in your pants, but you can't live without a liver and they can't transplant it either. That man was dead. Two years at the most, I gave him. Two years, all because he was in a bad mood and lurched his bus to trip up a smartmouth kid.

I felt like piss on a flat rock. On that day I had gone nearly eight months, since before Christmas, the whole *year* so far without hurting anybody. It was the best I'd ever done, and I thought I'd licked it. I stepped across the lady I smashed into and sat by the window, looking out, not seeing anything. All I could think was I'm sorry I'm sorry I'm sorry. Did he have a wife and kids? Well, they'd be a widow and orphans soon enough, because of me. I could feel him from clear over here. The sparkiness of his belly, making the cancer grow and keeping his body's own natural fire from burning it out. I wanted with all my heart to take it back, but I couldn't. And like so many times before, I thought to myself that if I had any guts I'd kill myself. I couldn't figure why I hadn't died of my own cancer already. I sure enough hated myself a lot worse than I ever hated anybody else.

The lady beside me starts to talk. "People like that are so annoying, aren't they?"

I didn't want to talk to anybody, so I just grunted and turned away.

"That was very kind of you to help me," she says.

That's when I realized she was the same lady who didn't have the right fare. "Nothing," I says.

"No, you didn't have to do that." She touched my jeans.

I turned to look at her. She was older, about twenty-five maybe, and her face looked kind of sweet. She was dressed nice enough that I could tell it wasn't cause she was poor that she didn't have bus fare. She also didn't take her hand off my knee, which made me nervous, because the bad thing I do is a lot stronger when I'm actually touching a person, and so I mostly don't touch folks and I don't feel safe when they touch me. The fastest I ever killed a man was when he felt me up in a bathroom at a rest stop on I-85. He was coughing blood when I left that place, I really tore him up that time, I still have nightmares about him gasping for breath there with his hand on me.

So anyway that's why I felt real nervous her touching me there on the bus, even though there was no harm in it. Or anyway that's half why I was nervous, and the other half was that her hand was real light on my leg and out of the corner of my eye I could see how her chest moved when she breathed, and after all I'm seventeen and normal most ways. So when I wished she'd move her hand, I only *half* wished she'd move it back to her own lap.

That was up till she smiles at me and says, "Mick, I want to help you."

It took me a second to realize she spoke my name. I didn't know many people in Roanoke, and she sure wasn't one of them. Maybe she was one of Mr. Kaiser's customers, I thought. But they hardly ever knew my name. I kind of thought, for a second, that maybe she had seen me working in the warehouse and asked Mr. Kaiser all about me or something. So I says, "Are you one of Mr. Kaiser's customers?"

"Mick Winger," she says. "You got your first

name from a note pinned to your blanket when you were left at the door of the sewage plant in Eden. You chose your last name when you ran away from the Eden Baptist Children's Home, and you probably chose it because the first movie you ever saw was *An Officer and a Gentleman*. You were fifteen then, and now you're seventeen, and you've killed more people in your life than Al Capone."

I got nervous when she knew my whole name and how I got it, cause the only way she could know that stuff was if she'd been following me for years. But when she let on she knew I killed people, I forgot all about feeling mad or guilty or horny. I pulled the cord on the bus, practically crawled over her to get out, and in about three seconds I was off that bus and hit the ground running. I'd been afraid of it for years, somebody finding out about me. But it was all the more scary seeing how she must have known about me for so *long*. It made me feel like somebody'd been peeking in the bathroom window all my life and I only just now found out about it.

I ran for a long time, which isn't easy because of all the hills in Roanoke. I ran mostly downhill, though, into town, where I could dodge into buildings and out their back doors. I didn't know if she was following me, but she'd been following me for a long time, or someone had, and I never even guessed it, so how did I know if they was following me now or not?

And while I ran, I tried to figure where I could go now. I had to leave town, that was sure. I couldn't go back to the warehouse, not even to say good-bye, and that made me feel real bad, cause Mr. Kaiser would think I just ran off for no reason, like some kid who didn't care nothing about people counting on him. He might even worry about me, never coming to pick up my spare clothes from the room he let me sleep in.

Thinking about what Mr. Kaiser might think about me going was pretty strange. Leaving Roanoke wasn't going to be like leaving the orphanage, and then leaving Eden, and finally leaving North Carolina. I never had much to let go of in those places. But Mr. Kaiser had always been real straight with me, a nice steady old guy, never bossed me, never tried to take me down, even stuck up for me in a quiet kind of way by letting it be known that he didn't want nobody teasing me. Hired me a year and a half ago, even though I was lying about being sixteen and he must've known it. And in all that time, I never once got mad at work, or at least not so mad I couldn't stop myself from hurting people. I worked hard, built up muscles I never thought I'd have, and I also must've grown five inches, my pants kept getting so short. I sweated and I ached most days after work, but I earned my pay and kept up with the older guys, and Mr. Kaiser never once made me feel like he took me on for charity, the way the orphanage people always did, like I should thank them for not letting me starve. Kaiser's Furniture Warehouse was the first peaceful place I ever spent time, the first place where nobody died who was my fault.

I knew all that before, but right till I started running I never realized how bad I'd feel about leaving Roanoke. Like somebody dying. It got so bad that for a while I couldn't hardly see which way I was going, not that I out-and-out cried or nothing.

Pretty soon I found myself walking down Jefferson Street, where it cuts through a woody hill before it widens out for car dealers and Burger Kings. There was cars passing me both ways, but I was thinking about other things now. Trying to figure why I never got mad at Mr. Kaiser. Other people treated me nice before, it wasn't like I got beat up every night or nobody ever gave me seconds or I had to eat dogfood or nothing. I remembered all those people at the orphanage, they was just trying to make me grow up Christian and educated. They just never learned how to be nice without also being nasty. Like Old Peleg, the black caretaker, he was a nice old coot and told us stories, and I never let nobody call him nigger even behind his back. But he was a racist himself, and I knew it on account of the time he caught me and Jody Capel practicing who could stop pissing the most times in a single go. We both done the same thing, didn't we? But he just sent me off and then started whaling on Jody, and Jody was yelling like he was dying, and I kept saying, "It ain't fair! I done it too! You're only beating on him cause he's black!" but he paid no mind, it was so crazy, I mean it wasn't like I wanted him to beat me too, but it made me so *mad* and before I knew it, I felt so sparky that I couldn't hold it in and I was

hanging on him, trying to pull him away from
Jody, so it hit him hard.

What could I say to him then? Going into the
hospital, where he'd lie there with a tube in his
arm and a tube in his nose sometimes. He told me
stories when he could talk, and just squoze my
hand when he couldn't. He used to have a belly
on him, but I think I could have tossed him in the
air like a baby before he died. And I did it to him,
not that I meant to, I couldn't help myself, but
that's the way it was. Even people I purely loved,
they'd have mean days, and God help them if I
happened to be there, because I was like God with
a bad mood, that's what I was, God with no mercy,
because I couldn't give them nothing, but I sure
as hell could take away. Take it all away. They
told me I shouldn't visit Old Peleg so much cause
it was sick to keep going to watch him waste away.
Mrs. Howard and Mr. Dennis both got tumors
from trying to get me to stop going. So many people was dying of cancer in those days they came
from the county and tested the water for chemicals. It wasn't no chemicals, I knew that, but I
never did tell them, cause they'd just lock me up
in the crazy house and you can bet that crazy
house would have a *epidemic* before I been there
a week if that ever happened.

Truth was I didn't know, I just didn't know it
was me doing it for the longest time. It's just people kept dying on me, everybody I ever loved, and
it seemed like they always took sick after I'd been
real mad at them once, and you know how little
kids always feel guilty about yelling at somebody

who dies right after. The counselor even told me that those feelings were perfectly natural, and of course it wasn't my fault, but I couldn't shake it. And finally I began to realize that other people didn't feel that sparky feeling like I did, and they couldn't tell how folks was feeling unless they looked or asked. I mean, I knew when my lady teachers was going to be on the rag before *they* did, and you can bet I stayed away from them the best I could on those crabby days. I could feel it, like they was giving off sparks. And there was other folks who had a way of sucking you to them, without saying a thing, without doing a thing, you just went into a room and couldn't take your eyes off them, you wanted to be close—I saw that other kids felt the same way, just automatically liked them, you know? But I could feel it like they was on fire, and suddenly I was cold and needed to warm myself. And I'd say something about it and people would look at me like I was crazy enough to lock right up, and I finally caught on that I was the only one that had those feelings.

Once I knew that, then all those deaths began to fit together. All those cancers, those days they lay in hospital beds turning into mummies before they was rightly dead, all the pain until they drugged them into zombies so they wouldn't tear their own guts out just trying to get to the place that hurt so bad. Torn up, cut up, drugged up, radiated, bald, skinny, praying for death, and I knew I did it. I began to tell the minute I did it. I began to know what kind of cancer it would be, and where, and how bad. And I was always right.

Twenty-five people I knew of, and probably more I didn't.

And it got even worse when I ran away. I'd hitch rides because how else was I going to get anywheres? But I was always scared of the people who picked me up, and if they got weird or anything I sparked them. And cops who run me out of a place, they got it. Until I figured I was just Death himself, with his bent-up spear and a hood over his head, walking around and whoever came near him bought the farm. That was me. I was the most terrible thing in the world, I was families broke up and children orphaned and mamas crying for their dead babies, I was everything that people hate most in all the world. I jumped off a overpass once to kill myself but I just sprained my ankle. Old Peleg always said I was like a cat, I wouldn't die lessen somebody skinned me, roasted the meat and ate it, then tanned the hide, made it into slippers, wore them slippers clean out, and then burned them and raked the ashes, that's when I'd finally die. And I figure he's right, cause I'm still alive and that's a plain miracle after the stuff I been through lately.

Anyway that's the kind of thing I was thinking, walking along Jefferson, when I noticed that a car had driven by going the other way and saw me and turned around and came back up behind me, pulled ahead of me and stopped. I was so spooked I thought it must be that lady finding me again, or maybe somebody with guns to shoot me all up like on "Miami Vice," and I was all set to take off up the hill till I saw it was just Mr. Kaiser.

He says, "I was heading the other way, Mick. Want a ride to work?"

I couldn't tell him what I was doing. "Not today, Mr. Kaiser," I says.

Well, he knew by my look or something, cause he says, "You quitting on me, Mick?"

I was just thinking, don't argue with me or nothing, Mr. Kaiser, just let me go, I don't want to hurt you, I'm so fired up with guilt and hating myself that I'm just death waiting to bust out and blast somebody, can't you see sparks falling off me like spray off a wet dog? I just says, "Mr. Kaiser, I don't want to talk right now, I really don't."

Right then was the moment for him to push. For him to lecture me about how I had to learn responsibility, and if I didn't talk things through how could anybody ever make things right, and life ain't a free ride so sometimes you got to do things you don't want to do, and I been nicer to you than you deserve, you're just what they warned me you'd be, shiftless and ungrateful and a bum in your soul.

But he didn't say none of that. He just says, "You had some bad luck? I can advance you against wages, I know you'll pay back."

"I don't owe no money," I says.

And he says, "Whatever you're running away from, come home with me and you'll be safe."

What could I say? You're the one who needs protecting, Mr. Kaiser, and I'm the one who'll probably kill you. So I didn't say nothing, until finally he just nodded and put his hand on my shoulder and said, "That's okay, Mick. If you ever need a place or a job, you just come on back to me. You find a place to settle down for a while, you write to me and I'll send you your stuff."

"You just give it to the next guy," I says.

"A son-of-a-bitch stinking mean old Jew like me?" he says. "I don't give nothing to nobody."

Well I couldn't help but laugh, cause that's what the foreman always called Mr. Kaiser whenever he thought the old guy couldn't hear him. And when I laughed, I felt myself cool off, just like as if I had been on fire and somebody poured cold water over my head.

"Take care of yourself, Mick," he says. He give me his card and a twenty and tucked it into my pocket when I told him no. Then he got back into his car and made one of his insane U-turns right across traffic and headed back the other way.

Well if he did nothing else he got my brain back in gear. There I was walking along the highway where anybody at all could see me, just like Mr. Kaiser did. At least till I was out of town I ought to stay out of sight as much as I could. So there I was between those two hills, pretty steep, and all covered with green, and I figured I could climb either one. But the slope on the other side of the road looked somehow better to me, it looked more like I just ought to go there, and I figured that was as good a reason to decide as any I ever heard of, and so I dodged my way across Jefferson Street and went right into the kudzu caves and clawed my way right up. It was dark under the leaves, but it wasn't much cooler than right out in the sun, particularly cause I was working so hard. It was a long way up, and just when I got to the top the ground started shaking. I thought it was an earthquake I was so edgy, till I heard the train whistle and then I knew it was one of those coal-hauling trains, so heavy it could shake ivy off a wall when it passed. I just stood there and listened to it, the sound coming from every direction all at once, there under the kudzu, I listened till it went on by, and then I stepped out of the leaves into a clearing.

And there she was, waiting for me, sitting under a tree.

I was too wore out to run, and too scared, coming on her sudden like that, just when I thought I was out of sight. It was just as if I'd been aiming straight at her, all the way up the hill, just as if she somehow tied a string to me and pulled me across the street and up the hill. And if she could do that, how could I run away from her, tell me that? Where could I go? I'd just turn some corner and there she'd be, waiting. So I says to her, "All right, what do you want?"

She just waved me on over. And I went, too, but not very close, cause I didn't know what she had in mind. "Sit down, Mick," says she. "We need to talk."

Now I'll tell you that I didn't want to sit, and I didn't want to talk, I just wanted to get out of there. And so I did, or at least I thought I did. I started walking straight away from her, I thought, but in three steps I realized that I wasn't walking away, I was walking around her. Like that planet thing in science class, the more I moved, the more

I got nowhere. It was like she had more say over what my legs did than me.

So I sat down.

"You shouldn't have run off from me," she says.

What I mostly thought of now was to wonder if she was wearing anything under that shirt. And then I thought, what a stupid time to be thinking about that. But I still kept thinking about it.

"Do you promise to stay right there till I'm through talking?" she says.

When she moved, it was like her clothes got almost transparent for a second, but not quite. Couldn't take my eyes off her. I promised.

And then all of a sudden she was just a woman. Not ugly, but not all that pretty, neither. Just looking at me with eyes like fire. I was scared again, and I wanted to leave, especially cause now I began to think she really was doing something to me. But I promised, so I stayed.

"That's how it began," she says.

"What's how what began?" says I.

"What you just felt. What I made you feel. That only works on people like you. Nobody else can feel it."

"Feel what?" says I. Now, I knew what she meant, but I didn't know for sure if she meant what I knew. I mean, it bothered me real bad that she could tell how I felt about her those few minutes there.

"Feel that," she says, and there it is again, all I can think about is her body. But it only lasted a few seconds, and then I knew for sure that she was doing it to me.

"Stop it," I says, and she says, "I already did."

I ask her, "How do you do that?"

"Everybody can do it, just a little. A woman looks at a man, she's interested, and so the bio-electrical system heats up, causes some odors to change, and he smells them and notices her and he pays attention."

"Does it work the other way?"

"Men are always giving off those odors, Mick. Makes no difference. It isn't a man's stink that gives a woman her ideas. But like I said, Mick, that's what everybody can do. With some men, though, it isn't a woman's smell that draws his eye. It's the bio-electrical system itself. The smell is nothing. You can feel the heat of the fire. It's the same thing as when you kill people, Mick. If you couldn't kill people the way you do, you also couldn't feel it so strong when I give off magnetic pulses."

Of course I didn't understand all that the first time, and maybe I'm remembering it now with words she didn't teach me until later. At the time, though, I was scared, yes, because she knew, and because she could do things to me, but I was also excited, because she sounded like she had some answers, like she knew why it was that I killed people without meaning to.

But when I asked her to explain everything, she couldn't. "We're only just beginning to understand it ourselves, Mick. There's a Swedish scientist who is making some strides that way. We've sent some people over to meet with him. We've read his book, and maybe even some of us understand it. I've got to tell you, Mick, just because we can do this thing doesn't mean that we're particularly smart or anything. It doesn't get us through college any faster or anything. It just means that teachers who flunk us tend to die off a little younger."

"You're like me! You can do it too!"

She shook her head. "Not likely," she says. "If I'm really furious at somebody, if I really hate him, if I really *try*, and if I keep it up for weeks, I can maybe give him an ulcer. You're in a whole different league from me. You and your people."

"I got no people," I says.

"I'm here, Mick, because you got people. People who knew just exactly what you could do from the minute you were born. People who knew that if you didn't get a tit to suck you wouldn't just cry, you'd kill. Spraying out death from your cradle. So they planned it all from the beginning. Put you in an orphanage. Let other people, all those do-gooders, let them get sick and die, and then when you're old enough to have control over it, then they look you up, they tell you who you are, they bring you home to live with them."

"So you're my kin?" I ask her.

"Not so you'd notice," she says. "I'm here to warn you about your kin. We've been watching you for years, and now it's time to warn you."

"*Now* it's time? I spent fifteen years in that children's home killing everybody who ever cared about me, and if they'd just come along—or you, or anybody, if you just said, Mick, you got to control your temper or you'll hurt people, if somebody just said to me, Mick, we're your people and we'll keep you safe, then maybe I wouldn't be so scared all the time, maybe I wouldn't go killing people so much, did you ever think of that?" Or maybe I didn't say all that, but that's what I was feeling, and so I said a lot, I chewed her up and down.

And then I saw how scared she was, because I was all sparky, and I realized I was just about to shed a load of death onto her, and so I kind of jumped back and yelled at her to leave me alone, and then she does the craziest thing, she reaches out toward me, and I scream at her, "Don't you touch me!" cause if she touches me I can't hold it in, it'll just go all through her and tear up her guts inside, but she just keeps reaching, leaning toward me, and so I kind of crawled over toward a tree, and I hung onto that tree, I just held on and let the tree kind of soak up all my sparkiness, almost like I was burning up the tree. Maybe I killed it, for all I know. Or maybe it was so big, I couldn't hurt it, but it took all the fire out of me, and then she *did* touch me, like nobody ever touched me, her arm across my back, and hand holding my shoulder, her face right up against my ear, and she says to me, "Mick, you didn't hurt me."

"Just leave me alone," says I.

"You're not like them," she says. "Don't you see that? They love the killing. They *use* the killing. Only they're not as strong as you. They have to be touching, for one thing, or close to it. They have to keep it up longer. They're stronger than *I* am, but not as strong as you. So they'll want you, that's for sure, Mick, but they'll also be scared of you, and you know what'll scare them most? That you didn't kill me, that you can *control* it like that."

"I can't always. That bus driver today."

"So you're not perfect. But you're trying. Trying not to kill people. Don't you see, Mick? You're not like them. They may be your blood family, but you don't belong with them, and they'll see that, and when they do—"

All I could think about was what she said, my blood family. "My mama and daddy, you telling me I'm going to meet them?"

"They're calling you now, and that's why I had to warn you."

"Calling me?"

"The way I called you up this hill. Only it wasn't just me, of course, it was a bunch of us."

"I just decided to come up here, to get off the road."

"You just decided to cross the highway and climb this hill, instead of the other one? Anyway, that's how it works. It's part of the human race for all time, only we never knew it. A bunch of people kind of harmonize their bio-electrical systems, to call for somebody to come home, and they come home, after a while. Or sometimes a whole nation unites to hate somebody. Like Iran and the Shah, or the Philippines and Marcos."

"They just kicked them out," I says.

"But they were already dying, weren't they? A whole nation, hating together, they make a constant interference with their enemy's bio-electrical system. A constant noise. All of them together, millions of people, they are finally able to match what you can do with one flash of anger."

I thought about that for a few minutes, and it came back to me all the times I thought how I wasn't even human. So maybe I *was* human, after all, but human like a guy with three arms is human, or one of those guys in the horror movies I saw, gigantic and lumpy and going around hacking up teenagers whenever they was about to get laid. And in all those movies they always try to kill the guy only they can't, he gets stabbed and shot and burned up and he still comes back, and that's like me, I must have tried to kill myself so many times only it never worked.

No. Wait a minute.

I got to get this straight, or you'll think I'm crazy or a liar. I didn't jump off that highway overpass like I said. I stood on one for a long time, watching the cars go by. Whenever a big old semi came along I'd say, this one, and I'd count, and at the right second I'd say, now. Only I never did jump. And then afterward I dreamed about jumping, and in all those dreams I'd just bounce off the truck and get up and limp away. Like the time I was a kid and sat in the bathroom with the little gardening shears, the spring-loaded kind that popped open, I sat there thinking about jamming it into my stomach right under the breastbone, and then letting go of the handle, it'd pop right open and make a bad wound and cut open my heart or something. I was there so long I fell asleep on the toilet, and later I dreamed about doing it but no blood ever came out, because I couldn't die.

So I never tried to kill myself. But I thought about it all the time. I was like those monsters in those movies, just killing people but secretly hoping somebody would catch on to what was going on and kill me first.

And so I says to her, "Why didn't you just kill me?"

And there she was with her face close to mine and she says, just like it was love talk, she says, "I've had you in my rifle sights, Mick, and then I didn't do it. Because I saw something in you. I saw that maybe you were trying to control it. That maybe you didn't want to use your power to kill. And so I let you live, thinking that one day I'd be here like this, telling you what you are, and giving you a little hope."

I thought she meant I'd hope because of knowing my mama and daddy were alive and wanted me.

"I hoped for a long time, but I gave it up. I don't want to see my mama and daddy, if they could leave me there all those years. I don't want to see you, neither, if you didn't so much as warn me not to get mad at Old Peleg. I didn't want to kill Old Peleg, and I couldn't even help it! You didn't help me a bit!"

"We argued about it," she says. "We knew you were killing people while you tried to sort things out and get control. Puberty's the worst time, even worse than infancy, and we knew that if we didn't kill you a lot of people would die—and mostly they'd be the people you loved best. That's the way it is for most kids your age, they get angriest at the people they love most, only you couldn't help killing them, and what does that do to your mind? What kind of person do you become? There was some who said we didn't have the right to leave you alive even to study you, because it would be like having a cure for cancer and then not using it on people just to see how fast they'd die. Like that experiment where the government left syphilis cases untreated just to see what the final stages of the disease were like, even though they could have cured those people at any time. But some of us told them, Mick isn't a disease, and a bullet isn't penicillin. I told them, Mick is something special. And they said, yes, he's special, he kills more than any of those other kids, and we shot *them* or ran them over with a truck or drowned them, and here we've got the worst one of all and you want to keep him alive."

And I was crying cause I wished they *had* killed me, but also because it was the first time I ever thought there was people arguing that I ought to be alive, and even though I didn't rightly understand then or even now why you didn't kill me, I got to tell you that knowing somebody knew what I was and still chose not to blast my head off, that done me in, I just bawled like a baby.

One thing led to another, there, my crying and her holding me, and pretty soon I figured out that she pretty much wanted to get laid right there. But that just made me sick, when I knew that. "How can you want to do that!" I says to her. "I can't get married! I can't have no kids! They'd be like me!"

She didn't argue with me or say nothing about birth control, and so I figured out later that I was right, she wanted to have a baby, and that told me plain that she was crazy as a loon. I got my pants pulled back up and my shirt on, and I wouldn't look at her getting dressed again, neither.

"I could make you do it," she says to me. "I could do that to you. The ability you have that lets you kill also makes you sensitive. I can make you lose your mind with desire for me."

"Then why don't you?" I says.

"Why don't you kill if you can help it?" she says.

"Cause nobody has the right," says I.

"That's right," she says.

"Anyway you're ten years older than me," I tell her.

"Fifteen," she says. "Almost twice your age. But that don't mean nothing." Or I guess she actually said, "That *doesn't* mean nothing," or probably, "That doesn't mean *anything*." She talks better than I do but I can't always remember the fancy way. "That doesn't mean a thing," she says. "You'll go to your folks, and you can bet they'll have some pretty little girl waiting for you, and she'll know how to do it much better than me, she'll turn you on so your pants unzip themselves, cause that's what they want most from you. They want your babies. As many as they can get, because you're the strongest they've produced in all the years since Grandpa Jake realized that the cursing power went father to son, mother to daughter, and that he could breed for it like you breed dogs or horses. They'll breed you like a stud, but then when they find out that you don't like killing people and you don't want to play along and you aren't going to take orders from whoever's in charge there now, they'll kill you. That's why I came to warn you. We could feel them just starting to call you. We knew it was time. And I came to warn you."

Most of this didn't mean much to me yet. Just the idea of having kinfolk was still so new I couldn't exactly get worried about whether they'd kill me or put me out for stud or whatever. Mostly what I thought about was her, anyway. "I might have killed you, you know."

"Maybe I didn't care," she says. "And maybe I'm not so easy to kill."

"And maybe you ought to tell me your name," says I.

"Can't," she says.

"How come?" says I.

"Because if you decide to put in with them, and you know my name, then I *am* dead."

"I wouldn't let anybody hurt you," says I.

She didn't answer that. She just says to me, "Mick, you don't know my name, but you remember this. I have hopes for you, cause I know you're a good man and you never meant to kill nobody. I could've made you love me, and I didn't, because I want you to do what you do by your own choice. And most important of all, if you come with me, we have a chance to see if maybe your ability doesn't have a good side."

You think I hadn't thought of that before? When

I saw Rambo shooting down all those little brown guys, I thought, I could do that, and without no gun, either. And if somebody took me hostage like the Achille Lauro thing, we wouldn't have to worry about the terrorists going unpunished. They'd all be rotting in a hospital in no time. "Are you with the government?" I ask her.

"No," she says.

So they didn't want me to be a soldier. I was kind of disappointed. I kind of thought I might be useful that way. But I couldn't volunteer or nothing, cause you don't walk into the recruiting office and say, I've killed a couple dozen people by giving sparks off my body, and I could do it to Castro and Qaddafi if you like. Cause if they believe you, then you're a murderer, and if they don't believe you, they lock you up in a nuthouse.

"Nobody's been calling me, anyway," I says. "If I didn't see you today, I wouldn't've gone nowhere. I would've stayed with Mr. Kaiser."

"Then why did you take all your money out of the bank?" she says. "And when you ran away from me, why did you run toward the highway where you can hitch a ride at least to Madison and then catch another on in to Eden?"

And I didn't have no answer for her then, cause I didn't know rightly why I took my money out of the bank lessen it was like she said, and I was planning to leave town. It was just an impulse, to close that account, I didn't think nothing of it, just stuffed three hundreds into my wallet and come to think of it I really was heading toward

Eden, I just didn't *think* of it, I was just *doing* it. Just the way I climbed up that hill.

"They're stronger than we are," she says. "So we can't hold you here. You have to go anyway, you have to work this thing out. The most we could do was just get you on the bus next to me, and then call you up this hill."

"Then why don't you come with me?" I says.

"They'd kill me in two seconds, right in front of your eyes, and none of this cursing stuff, either, Mick. They'd just take my head off with a machete."

"Do they know you?"

"They know *us*," she says. "We're the only ones that know your people exist, so we're the only ones working to stop them. I won't lie to you, Mick. If you join them, you can find us, you'll learn how, it isn't hard, and you can do this stuff from farther away, you could really take us apart. But if you join *us*, the tables are turned."

"Well maybe I don't want to be on either side in this war," I says. "And maybe now I won't go to Eden, neither. Maybe I'll go up to Washington, D.C. and join the CIA."

"Maybe," she says.

"And don't try to stop me."

"I wouldn't try," she says.

"Damn straight," I says. And then I just walked on out, and this time I didn't walk in no circles, I just headed north, past her car, down the railroad right of way. And I caught a ride heading up toward D.C., and that was that.

Except that along about six o'clock in the evening I woke up and the car was stopping and I didn't know where I was, I must have slept all day, and the guy says to me, "Here you are, Eden, North Carolina."

And I about messed my pants. "Eden!" I says.

"It wasn't far out of my way," he says. "I'm heading for Burlington, and these country roads are nicer than the freeway, anyway. Don't mind if I never drive I-85 again, to tell the truth."

But that was the very guy who told me he had business in D.C., he was heading there from Bristol, had to see somebody from a government agency, and here he was in Eden. It made no sense at all, except for what that woman told me. Somebody was calling me, and if I wouldn't come, they'd just put me to sleep and call whoever was driving. And there I was. Eden, North Carolina. Scared to death, or at least scared a little, but also thinking, if what she said was true, my folks was coming, I was going to meet my folks.

Nothing much changed in the two years since I ran off from the orphanage. Nothing much ever changes in Eden, which isn't a real town anyway, just cobbled together from three little villages that combined to save money on city services. People still mostly think of them as three villages. There wasn't nobody who'd get too excited about seeing me, and there wasn't nobody I wanted to see. Nobody living, anyway. I had no idea how my folks might find me, or how I might find them, but in the meantime I went to see about the only people I ever much cared about. Hoping that they wouldn't rise up out of the grave to get even with me for killing them.

It was still full day that time of year, but it was whippy weather, the wind gusting and then holding still, a big row of thunderclouds off to the southwest, the sun sinking down to get behind them. The kind of afternoon that promises to cool you off, which suited me fine. I was still pretty dusty from my climb up the hill that morning, and I could use a little rain. Got a Coke at a fast food place and then walked on over to see Old Peleg.

He was buried in a little cemetery right by an old Baptist Church. Not Southern Baptist, *Black* Baptist, meaning that it didn't have no fancy building with classrooms and a rectory, just a stark-white block of a building with a little steeple and a lawn that looked like it'd been clipped by hand. Cemetery was just as neat-kept. Nobody around, and it was dim cause of the thunderclouds moving through, but I wasn't afraid of the graves there, I just went to Old Peleg's cross. Never knew his last name was Lindley. Didn't sound like a black man's name, but then when I thought about it I realized that *no* last name sounded like a black man's name, because Eden is still just old-fashioned enough that an old black man doesn't get called by his last name much. He grew up in a Jim Crow state, and never got around to insisting on being called Mr. Lindley. Old Peleg. Not that he ever hugged me or took me on long walks or gave me that tender loving care that makes people get all teary-eyed about how wonderful it is to have parents. He never tried to be my dad or nothing. And if I hung around him much, he always gave me work to do and made damn sure I did it right, and mostly we didn't talk about anything except the work we was doing, which made me wonder, standing there, why I wanted to cry and why I hated myself worse for killing Old Peleg than for any of the other dead people under the ground in that city.

I didn't see them and I didn't hear them coming and I didn't smell my mama's perfume. But I knew they was coming, because I felt the prickly air between us. I didn't turn around, but I knew just where they were, and just how far off, because they was *lively*. Shedding sparks like I never saw on any living soul except myself, just walking along giving off light. It was like seeing myself from the outside for the first time in my life. Even when she was making me get all hot for her, that lady in Roanoke wasn't as lively as them. They was just like me.

Funny thing was, that wrecked everything. I didn't want them to be like me. I *hated* my sparkiness, and there they were, showing it to me, making me see how a killer looks from the outside. It took a few seconds to realize that they was *scared* of me, too. I recognized how scaredness looks, from remembering how my own bio-electrical system got shaped and changed by fear. Course I didn't think of it as a bio-electrical system then, or maybe I did cause she'd already told me, but you know what I mean. They was afraid of me. And I knew that was because I was giving off all the sparks I shed when I feel so mad at myself that I could bust. I was standing there at Old Peleg's grave, hating myself, so naturally they saw me like I was ready to kill half a city. They didn't know that it was me I was hating. Naturally they figured I might be mad at *them* for leaving me at that orphanage seventeen years ago. Serve them right, too, if I gave them a good hard twist in the gut, but I don't do that, I honestly don't, not any more, not standing there by Old Peleg who I loved a lot more than these two strangers, I don't act out being a murderer when my shadow's falling across his grave.

So I calmed myself down as best I could and I turned around and there they was, my mama and my daddy. And I got to tell you I almost laughed. All those years I watched them TV preachers, and we used to laugh till our guts ached about how Tammy Bakker always wore makeup so thick she could be a nigger underneath (it was okay to say that cause Old Peleg himself said it first) and here was my mama, wearing just as much makeup and her hair sprayed so thick she could work construction without a hardhat. And smiling that same sticky phony smile, and crying the same gooey oozey black tears down her cheeks, and reaching out her hands just the right way so I halfway expected her to say, "Praise to Lord Jesus," and then she actually *says* it, "Praise to Lord Jesus, it's my boy," and comes up and lays a kiss on my cheek with so much spit in it that it dripped down my face.

I wiped the slobber with my sleeve and felt my

daddy have this little flash of anger, and I knew that he thought I was judging my mama and he didn't like it. Well, I was, I got to admit. Her perfume was enough to knock me over, I swear she must've mugged an Avon lady. And there was my daddy in a fine blue suit like a businessman, his hair all blow-dried, so it was plain he knew just as well as I did the way real people are supposed to look. Probably he was plain embarrassed to be seen in public with Mama, so why didn't he ever just say, Mama, you wear too much makeup? That's what I thought, and it wasn't till later that I realized that when your woman is apt to give you cancer if you rile her up, you don't go telling her that her face looks like she slept in wet sawdust and she smells like a whore. White trash, that's what my mama was, sure as if she was still wearing the factory label.

"Sure am glad to see you, Son," says my daddy.

I didn't know what to say, tell the truth. I *wasn't* glad to see them, now that I saw them, because they wasn't exactly what a orphan boy dreams his folks is like. So I kind of grinned and looked back down at Old Peleg's grave.

"You don't seem too surprised to see *us*," he says.

I could've told him right then about the lady in Roanoke, but I didn't. Just didn't feel right to tell him. So I says, "I felt like somebody was calling me back here. And you two are the only people I met who's as sparky as me. If you all say you're my folks, then I figure it must be so."

Mama giggled and she says to him, "Listen, Jesse, he calls it 'sparky.' "

"The word we use is 'dusty,' Son," says Daddy. "We say a body's looking dusty when he's one of us."

"You were a very dusty baby," says Mama. "That's why we knew we couldn't keep you. Never seen such a dusty baby before. Papa Lem made us take you to the orphanage before you even sucked one time. You never sucked even once." And her mascara just flooded down her face.

"Now Deeny," says Daddy, "no need telling him everything right here."

Dusty. That was no sense at all. It didn't look like *dust*, it was flecks of light, so bright on me that sometimes I had to squint just to see my own hands through the dazzle. "It don't *look* like dust," I says.

And Daddy says, "Well what do *you* think it looks like?"

And I says, "Sparks. That's why I call it being sparky."

"Well that's what it looks like to us, too," says Daddy. "But we've been calling it 'dusty' all our lives, and so I figure it's easier for one boy to change than for f—for lots of other folks."

Well, now, I learned a lot of things right then from what he said. First off, I knew he was lying when he said it looked like sparks to them. It didn't. It looked like what they called it. Dust. And that meant that I was seeing it a whole lot *brighter* than they could see it, and that was good for me to know, especially because it was plain that Daddy *didn't* want me to know it and so he pretended that he saw it the same way. He wanted me to think he was just as good at seeing as I was. Which meant that he sure wasn't. And I also learned that he didn't want me to know how many kinfolk I had, cause he started to say a number that started with *F*, and then caught himself and didn't say it. Fifty? Five hundred? The number wasn't half so important as the fact that he didn't want me to know it. They didn't trust me. Well, why should they? Like the lady said, I was better at this than they were, and they didn't know how mad I was about being abandoned, and the last thing they wanted to do was turn me loose killing folks. Especially themselves.

Well I stood there thinking about that stuff and pretty soon it makes them nervous and Mama says, "Now, Daddy, he can call it whatever he wants, don't go making him mad or something."

And Daddy laughs and says, "He isn't mad, are you, Son?"

Can't they see for themselves? Course not. Looks like *dust* to them, so they can't see it clear at all.

"You don't seem too happy to see us," says Daddy.

"Now, Jesse," says Mama, "don't go pushing. Papa Lem said don't you push the boy, you just make his acquaintance, you let him know why we had to push him out of the nest so young, so now you explain it, Daddy, just like Papa Lem said to."

For the first time right then it occurred to me that my own folks didn't *want* to come fetch me. They came because this Papa Lem made them do it. And you can bet they hopped and said yes, knowing how Papa Lem used his—but I'll get to Papa Lem in good time, and you said I ought to take this all in order, which I'm mostly trying to do.

Anyway Daddy explained it just like the lady in Roanoke, except he didn't say a word about bioelectrical systems, he said that I was "plainly chosen" from the moment of my birth, that I was "one of the elect," which I remembered from Baptist Sunday School meant that I was one that God had saved, though I never heard of anybody who was saved the minute they was born and not even baptized or nothing. They saw how dusty I was and they knew I'd kill a lot of people before I got old enough to control it. I asked them if they did it a lot, putting a baby out to be raised by strangers.

"Oh, maybe a dozen times," says Daddy.

"And it always works out okay?" says I.

He got set to lie again, I could see it by ripples in the light, I didn't know lying could be so plain, which made me glad they saw dust instead of sparks. "Most times," he says.

"I'd like to meet one of them others," says I. "I figure we got a lot in common, growing up thinking our parents hated us, when the truth was they was scared of their own baby."

"Well they're mostly grown up and gone off," he says, but it's a lie, and most important of all was the fact that here I as much as said I thought they wasn't worth horse pucky as parents and the only thing Daddy can think of to say is why I can't see none of the other "orphans," which tells me that whatever he's lying to cover up must be real important.

But I didn't push him right then, I just looked back down at Old Peleg's grave and wondered if he ever told a lie in his life.

Daddy says, "I'm not surprised to find you here." I guess he was nervous, and had to change the subject. "He's one you dusted, isn't he?"

Dusted. That word made me so mad. What I done to Old Peleg wasn't *dusting*. And being mad must have changed me enough they could see the change. But they didn't know what it meant, cause Mama says to me, "Now, Son, I don't mean to criticize, but it isn't right to take pride in the gifts of God. That's why we came to find you, because we need to teach you why God chose you to be one of the elect, and you shouldn't glory in yourself because you could strike down your enemies. Rather you should give all glory to the Lord, praise his name, because we are his servants."

I like to puked, I was so mad at that. Glory! Old Peleg, who was worth ten times these two phony white people who tossed me out before I ever sucked tit, and they thought I should give the *glory* for his terrible agony and death to *God*? I didn't know God all that well, mostly because I thought of him as looking as pinched up and serious as Mrs. Bethel who taught Sunday School when I was little, until she died of leukemia, and I just never had a thing to say to God. But if God gave me that power to strike down Old Peleg, and God wanted the glory for it when I was done, then I *did* have a few words to say to God. Only I didn't believe it for a minute. Old Peleg believed in God, and the God he believed in didn't go striking an old black man dead because a dumb kid got pissed off at him.

But I'm getting off track in the story, because that was when my father touched me for the first time. His hand was shaking. And it had every right to shake, because I was so mad that a year ago he would've been bleeding from the colon before he took his hand away. But I'd got so I could keep from killing whoever touched me when I was mad, and the funny thing was that his hand *shaking* kind of changed how I felt anyway. I'd been thinking about how mad I was that they left me and how mad I was that they thought I'd be proud of killing people but now I realized how brave they was to come fetch me, cause how did they know I wouldn't kill them? But they came anyway. And that's something. Even if Papa Lem told them to do it, they came, and now I realized that it was real brave for Mama to come kiss me on the cheek right then, because if I was going to kill her, she touched me and gave me a chance to do it before she even tried to explain anything. Maybe it was her strategy to win me over or something, but it was still brave. And she also didn't approve of people being proud of murder, which was more points in her favor. And she had the guts to tell me so right to my face. So I chalked up some points for Mama. She might look like as sickening as

Tammy Bakker, but she faced her killer son with more guts than Daddy had.

He touched my shoulder and they led me to their car. A Lincoln Town Car, which they probably thought would impress me, but all I thought about was what it would've been like at the Children's Home if we'd had the price of that car, even fifteen years ago. Maybe a paved basketball court. Maybe some decent toys that wasn't broken-up hand-me-downs. Maybe some pants with knees in them. I never felt so poor in my life as when I slid onto that fuzzy seat and heard the stereo start playing elevator music in my ear.

There was somebody else in the car. Which made sense. If I'd killed them or something, they'd need somebody else to drive the car home, right? He wasn't much, when it came to being dusty or sparky or whatever. Just a little, and in rhythms of fear, too. And I could see *why* he was scared, cause he was holding a blindfold in his hands, and he says, "Mr. Yow, I'm afraid I got to put this on you."

Well, I didn't answer for a second, which made him more scared cause he thought I was mad, but mostly it took me that long to realize he meant *me* when he said "Mr. Yow."

"That's our name, Son," says my daddy. "I'm Jesse Yow, and your mother is Minnie Rae Yow, and that makes you Mick Yow."

"Don't it figure," says I. I was joking, but they took it wrong, like as if I was making fun of their name. But I been Mick Winger so long that it just feels silly calling myself Yow, and the fact is it *is* a funny name. They said it like I should be proud of it, though, which makes me laugh, but to them it was the name of God's Chosen People, like the way the Jews called themselves Israelites in the Bible. I didn't know that then, but that's the way they said it, real proud. And they was ticked off when I made a joke, so I helped them feel better by letting Billy put on—Billy's the name of the man in the car—put on the blindfold.

It was a lot of country roads, and a lot of country talk. About kinfolk I never met, and how I'd love this person and that person, which sounded increasingly unlikely to me, if you know what I mean. A long-lost child is coming home and you put a *blindfold* on him. I knew we were going mostly east, cause of the times I could feel the sun coming in my window and on the back of my neck, but that was about it, and that wasn't much. They lied to me, they wouldn't show me nothing, they was scared of me. I mean, any way you look at it, they wasn't exactly killing the fatted calf for the prodigal son. I was definitely on probation. Or maybe even on trial. Which, I might point out, is exactly the way you been treating me, too, and I don't like it much better now than I did then, if you don't mind me putting some personal complaints into this. I mean, somewhere along the line somebody's going to have to decide whether to shoot me or let me go, because I can't control my temper forever locked up like a rat in a box, and the difference is a rat can't reach out of the box and blast you the way I can, so somewhere along the way somebody's going to have to figure out that you better either trust me or kill me. My personal preference is for trusting me, since I've given you more reason to trust me than you've given me to trust *you* so far.

But anyway I rode along in the car for more than an hour. We could have gotten to Winston or Greensboro or Danville by then, it was so long, and by the time we got there nobody was talking and from the snoring, Billy was even asleep. I wasn't asleep, though. I was watching. Cause I don't see sparks with my eyes, I see it with something else, like as if my sparks see other folks' sparks, if you catch my drift, and so that blindfold might've kept me from seeing the road, but it sure didn't keep me from seeing the other folks in the car with me. I knew right where they were, and right what they were feeling. Now, I've always had a knack for telling things about people, even when I couldn't see nary a spark or nothing, but this was the first time I ever saw anybody who was sparky besides me. So I sat there watching how Mama and Daddy acted with each other even when they wasn't touching or saying a thing, just little drifts of anger or fear or—well, I looked for love, but I didn't see it, and I know what it looks like, cause I've felt it. They were like two armies camped on opposite hills, waiting for the truce to end at dawn. Careful. Sending out little scouting parties.

Then the more I got used to understanding what my folks was thinking and feeling, toward each other, the easier it got for me to read what Billy had going on inside him. It's like after you learn to read big letters, you can read little letters, too, and I wondered if maybe I could even learn to understand people who didn't have hardly any sparks at all. I mean that occurred to me, anyway, and since then I've found out that it's mostly true. Now that I've had some practice I can read a sparky person from a long ways off, and even regular folks I can do a little reading, even through walls and windows. But I found that out later. Like when you guys have been watching me through mirrors. I can also see your microphone wires in the walls.

Anyway it was during that car ride that I first started seeing what I could see with my eyes closed, the shape of people's bio-electrical system, the color and spin of it, the speed and the flow and the rhythm and whatever, I mean those are the words I use, cause there isn't exactly a lot of books I can read on the subject. Maybe that Swedish doctor has fancy words for it. I can only tell you how it feels to me. And in that hour I got to be good enough at it that I could tell Billy was scared, all right, but he *wasn't* all that scared of me, he was mostly scared of Mama and Daddy. Me he was jealous of, angry kind of. Scared a little, too, but mostly mad. I thought maybe he was mad cause I was coming in out of nowhere already sparkier than him, but then it occurred to me that he probably couldn't even tell how sparky I was, because to him it'd look like dust, and he wouldn't have enough of a knack at it to see much distinction between one person and another. It's like the more light you give off, the clearer you can see other people's light. So I was the one with the blindfold on, but I could see clearer than anybody else in that car.

We drove on gravel for about ten minutes, and then on a bumpy dirt road, and then suddenly on asphalt again, smooth as you please, for about a hundred yards, and then we stopped. I didn't wait for a by-your-leave, I had that blindfold off in half a second.

It was like a whole town of houses, but right among the trees, not a gap in the leaves overhead. Maybe fifty, sixty houses, some of them pretty big, but the trees made them half invisible, it being summer. Children running all over, scruffy dirty kids from diapered-up snot-nose brats to most-growed kids not all that much younger than me. They sure kept us cleaner in the Children's Home. And they was all sparky. Mostly like Billy, just a little, but it explained why they wasn't much washed. There isn't many a mama who'd stuff her kid in a tub if the kid can make her sick just by getting mad.

It must've been near eight-thirty at night, and even the little kids still wasn't in bed. They must let their kids play till they get wore out and drop down and fall asleep by themselves. It came to me that maybe I wasn't so bad off growing up in an orphanage. At least I knew manners and didn't whip it out and pee right in front of company, the way one little boy did, just looking at me while I got out of the car, whizzing away like he wasn't doing nothing strange. Like a dog marking trees.

He needed to so he done it. If I ever did that at the Children's Home they'd've slapped me silly.

I know how to act with strangers when I'm hitching a ride, but not when I'm being company, cause orphans don't go calling much so I never had much experience. So I'd've been shy no matter what, even if there wasn't no such thing as sparkiness. Daddy was all set to take me to meet Papa Lem right off, but Mama saw how I wasn't cleaned up and maybe she guessed I hadn't been to the toilet in a while and so she hustled me into a house where they had a good shower and when I came out she had a cold ham sandwich waiting for me on the table. On a plate, and the plate was setting on a linen place mat, and there was a tall glass of milk there, so cold it was sweating on the outside of the glass. I mean, if an orphan kid ever dreamed of what it might be like to have a mama, that was the dream. Never mind that she didn't look like a model in the Sears catalog. I felt clean, the sandwich tasted good, and when I was done eating she even offered me a cookie.

It felt good, I'll admit that, but at the same time I felt cheated. It was just too damn late. I needed it to be like this when I was seven, not seventeen.

But she was trying, and it wasn't all her fault, so I ate the cookie and drank off the last of the milk and my watch said it was after nine. Outside it was dusk now, and most of the kids were finally gone off to bed, and Daddy comes in and says, "Papa Lem says he isn't getting any younger."

He was outside, in a big rocking chair sitting on

the grass. You wouldn't call him fat, but he did have a belly on him. And you wouldn't call him old, but he was bald on top and his hair was wispy yellow and white. And you wouldn't call him ugly, but he had a soft mouth and I didn't like the way it twisted up when he talked.

Oh, hell, he was fat, old, and ugly, and I hated him from the first time I saw him. A squishy kind of guy. Not even as sparky as my daddy, neither, so you didn't get to be in charge around here just by having more of whatever it was made us different. I wondered how close kin he was to me. If he's got children, and they look like him, they ought to drown them out of mercy.

"Mick Yow," he says to me, "Mick my dear boy, Mick my dear cousin."

"Good evening, sir," says I.

"Oh, and he's got manners," says he. "We were right to donate so much to the Children's Home. They took excellent care of you."

"You donated to the home?" says I. If they did, they sure didn't give *much*.

"A little," he says. "Enough to pay for your food, your room, your Christian education. But no luxuries. You couldn't grow up soft, Mick. You had to grow up lean and strong. And you had to know suffering, so you could be compassionate. The Lord God has given you a marvelous gift, a great helping of his grace, a heaping plateful of the power of God, and we had to make sure you were truly worthy to sit up to the table at the banquet of the Lord."

I almost looked around to see if there was a

camera, he sounded so much like the preachers on TV.

And he says, "Mick, you have already passed the first test. You have forgiven your parents for leaving you to think you were an orphan. You have kept that holy commandment, Honor thy father and mother, that thy days may be long upon the land which the Lord thy God hath given thee. You know that if you had raised a hand against them, the Lord would have struck you down. For verily I say unto you that there was two rifles pointed at you the whole time, and if your father and mother had walked away without you, you would have flopped down dead in that nigger cemetery, for God will not be mocked."

I couldn't tell if he was trying to provoke me or scare me or what, but either way, it was working.

"The Lord has chosen you for his servant, Mick, just like he's chosen all of us. The rest of the world doesn't understand this. But Grandpa Jake saw it. Long ago, back in 1820, he saw how everybody he hated had a way of dying without him lifting a finger. And for a time he thought that maybe he was like those old witches, who curse people and they wither up and die by the power of the devil. But he was a god-fearing man, and he had no truck with Satan. He was living in rough times, when a man was likely to kill in a quarrel, but Grandpa Jake never killed. Never even struck out with his fists. He was a peaceable man, and he kept his anger inside him, as the Lord commands in the New Testament. So surely he was not a servant of Satan!"

Papa Lem's voice rang through that little village, he was talking so loud, and I noticed there was a bunch of people all around. Not many kids now, all grown-ups, maybe there to hear Lem, but even more likely they was there to see me. Because it was like the lady in Roanoke said, there wasn't a one of them was half as sparky as me. I didn't know if they could all see that, but *I* could. Compared to normal folks they was all dusty enough, I suppose, but compared to me, or even to my mama and daddy, they was a pretty dim bunch.

"He studied the scriptures to find out what it meant that his enemies all suffered from tumors and bleeding and coughing and rot, and he came upon the verse of Genesis where the Lord said unto Abraham, 'I will bless them that bless thee, and curse him that curseth thee.' And he knew in his heart that the Lord had chosen him the way he chose Abraham. And when Isaac gave the blessing of God to Jacob, he said, 'Let people serve thee, and nations bow down to thee: cursed be every one that curseth thee, and blessed be he that blesseth thee.' The promises to the patriarchs were fulfilled again in Grandpa Jake, for whoever cursed him was cursed by God."

When he said those words from the Bible, Papa Lem sounded like the voice of God himself, I've got to tell you. I felt exalted, knowing that it was God who gave such power to my family. It was to the whole family, the way Papa Lem told it, because the Lord promised Abraham that his children would be as many as there was stars in the sky, which is a lot more than Abraham knew about seeing how he didn't have no telescope. And that promise now applied to Grandpa Jake, just like the one that said "in thee shall all families of the earth be blessed." So Grandpa Jake set to studying the book of Genesis so he could fulfill those promises just like the patriarchs did. He saw how they went to a lot of trouble to make sure they only married kinfolk—you know how Abraham married his brother's daughter, Sarah, and Isaac married his cousin Rebekah, and Jacob married his cousins Leah and Rachel. So Grandpa Jake left his first wife cause she was unworthy, meaning she probably wasn't particularly sparky, and he took up with his brother's daughter and when his brother threatened to kill him if he laid a hand on the girl, Grandpa Jake run off with her and his own brother died of a curse which is just exactly what happened to Sarah's father in the Bible. I mean Grandpa Jake worked it out just right. And he made sure all his sons married their first cousins, and so all of them had sparkiness twice over, just like breeding pointers with pointers and not mixing them with other breeds, so the strain stays pure.

There was all kinds of other stuff about Lot and his daughters, and if we remained faithful then we would be the meek who inherit the Earth because we were the chosen people and the Lord would strike down everybody who stood in our way, but what it all came down to at the moment was this: You marry whoever the patriarch tells you to marry, and Papa Lem was the patriarch. He had my mama marry my daddy even though they never particularly liked each other, growing up cousins, because he could see that they was both specially chosen, which means to say they was both about the sparkiest there was. And when I was born, they knew it was like a confirmation of Papa Lem's decision, because the Lord had blessed them with a kid who gave off dust thicker than a dump truck on a dirt road.

One thing he asked me real particular was whether I ever been laid. He says to me, "Have you spilled your seed among the daughters of Ishmael and Esau?"

I knew what spilling seed was, cause we got lectures about that at the Children's Home. I wasn't sure who the daughters of Ishmael and Esau was, but since I never had a hot date, I figured I was pretty safe saying no. Still, I did consider a second, because what came to mind was the lady in Roanoke, stoking me up just by wanting me, and I was thinking about how close I'd come to not being a virgin after all. I wondered if the lady from Roanoke was a daughter of Esau.

Papa Lem picked up on my hesitation, and he wouldn't let it go. "Don't lie to me boy. I can see a lie." Well, since *I* could see a lie, I didn't doubt but what maybe he could too. But then again, I've had plenty of grown-ups tell me they could spot a lie—but half the time they accused me of lying when I was telling the truth, and the other half they believed me when I was telling whoppers so big it'd take two big men to carry them upstairs. So maybe he could and maybe he couldn't. I figured I'd tell him just as much truth as I wanted. "I was just embarrassed to tell you I never had a girl," I says.

"Ah, the deceptions of the world," he says. "They make promiscuity seem so normal that a boy is ashamed to admit that he is chaste." Then he got a glint in his eye. "I know the children of Esau have been watching you, wanting to steal your birthright. Isn't that so?"

"I don't know who Esau is," says I.

The folks who was gathered around us started muttering about that.

I says, "I mean, I know who he was in the Bible, he was the brother of Jacob, the one who sold him his birthright for split pea soup."

"Jacob was the rightful heir, the true eldest son," says Papa Lem, "and don't you forget it. Esau is the one who went away from his father, out into the wilderness, rejecting the things of God and embracing the lies and sins of the world. Esau is the one who married a strange woman, who was not of the people! Do you understand me?"

I understood pretty good by then. Somewhere along the line somebody got sick of living under the thumb of Papa Lem, or maybe the patriarch before him, and they split.

"Beware," says Papa Lem, "because the children of Esau and Ishmael still covet the blessings of Jacob. They want to corrupt the pure seed of Grandpa Jake. They have enough of the blessing of God to know that you're a remarkable boy, like Joseph who was sold into Egypt, and they will come to you with their whorish plans, the way

Potiphar's wife came to Joseph, trying to persuade you to give them your pure and undefiled seed so that they can have the blessing that their fathers rejected."

I got to tell you that I didn't much like having him talk about my seed so much in front of mixed company, but that was nothing compared to what he did next. He waved his hand to a girl standing there in the crowd, and up she came. She wasn't half bad-looking, in a country sort of way. Her hair was mousy and she wasn't altogether clean and she stood with a two-bucket slouch, but her face wasn't bad and she looked to have her teeth. Sweet, but not my type, if you know what I mean.

Papa Lem introduced us. It was his daughter, which I might've guessed, and then he says to her, "Wilt thou go with this man?" And she looks at me and says, "I will go." And then she gave me this big smile, and all of a sudden it was happening again, just like it did with the lady in Roanoke, only twice as much, cause after all the lady in Roanoke wasn't hardly sparky. I was standing there and all I could think about was how I wanted all her clothes off her and to do with her right there in front of everybody and I didn't even care that all those people were watching, that's how strong it was.

And I liked it, I got to tell you. I mean you don't ignore a feeling like that. But another part of me was standing back and it says to me, "Mick Winger you damn fool, that girl's as homely as the bathroom sink, and all these people are watching her make an idiot out of you," and it was that part of me that got mad, because I didn't like her making me do something, and I didn't like it happening right out in front of everybody, and I specially didn't like Papa Lem sitting there looking at his own daughter and me like we was in a dirty magazine.

Thing is, when I get mad I get all sparky, and the madder I got, the more I could see how she was doing it, like she was a magnet, drawing me to her. And as soon as I thought of it like us being magnets, I took all the sparkiness from being mad and I used it. Not to hurt her or nothing, because I didn't put it on her the way I did with the people I killed. I just kind of turned the path of her sparks plain upside down. She was spinning it just as fast as ever, but it went the other way, and the second that started, why, it was like she disappeared. I mean, I could see her all right, but I couldn't hardly *notice* her. I couldn't focus my eyes on her.

Papa Lem jumped right to his feet, and the other folks were gasping. Pretty quick that girl stopped sparking at me, you can bet, and there she was on her knees, throwing up. She must've had a real weak digestion, or else what I done was stronger than I thought. She was really pouring on the juice, I guess, and when I flung it back at her and turned her upside down, well, she couldn't hardly walk when they got her up. She was pretty hysterical, too, crying about how awful and ugly I was, which might've hurt my feelings except that I was scared to death.

Papa Lem was looking like the wrath of God. "You have rejected the holy sacrament of mar-

riage! You have spurned the handmaid God prepared for you!"

Now you've got to know that I hadn't put everything together yet, or I wouldn't have been so
afraid of him, but for all I knew right then he could
kill me with a cancer. And it was a sure thing he
could've had those people beat me to death or
whatever he wanted, so maybe I was right to be
scared. Anyway I had to think of a way to make
him not be mad at me, and what I came up with
must not've been too bad because it worked, didn't
it?

I says to him, as calm as I can, "Papa Lem,
she was not an acceptable handmaiden." I didn't
watch all those TV preachers for nothing. I knew
how to talk like the Bible. I says, "She was not
blessed enough to be my wife. She wasn't even as
blessed as my mama. You can't tell me that she's
the best the Lord prepared for me."

And sure enough, he calmed right down. "I
know that," he says. And he isn't talking like a
preacher any more, it's *me* talking like a preacher
and him talking all meek. "You think I don't know
it? It's those children of Esau, that's what it is,
Mick, you got to know that. We had five girls who
were a lot dustier than her, but we had to put them
out into other families, cause they were like you,
so strong they would've killed their own parents
without meaning to."

And I says, "Well, you brought me back, didn't
you?"

And he says, "Well you were *alive*, Mick, and
you got to admit that makes it easier."

"You mean those girls're all dead?" I says.

"The children of Esau," he says. "Shot three of them, strangled one, and we never found the body of the other. They never lived to be ten years old."

And I thought about how the lady in Roanoke told me she had me in her gunsights a few times. But she let me live. Why? For my seed? Those girls would've had seed too, or whatever. But they killed those girls and let me live. I didn't know why. Hell, I still don't, not if you mean to keep me locked up like this for the rest of my life. I mean you might as well have blasted my head off when I was six, and then I can name you a dozen good folks who'd still be alive, so no thanks for the favor if you don't plan to let me go.

Anyway, I says to him, "I didn't know that. I'm sorry."

And he says to me, "Mick, I can see how you'd be disappointed, seeing how you're so blessed by the Lord. But I promise you that my daughter is indeed the best girl of marriageable age that we've got here. I wasn't trying to foist her off on you because she's my daughter—it would be blasphemous for me to try it, and I'm a true servant of the Lord. The people here can testify for me, they can tell you that I'd never give you my own daughter unless she was the best we've got."

If she was the best they got then I had to figure the laws against inbreeding made pretty good sense. But I says to him, "Then maybe we ought to wait and see if there's somebody younger, too young to marry right now." I remembered the story of Jacob from Sunday School, and since they

set such store by Jacob I figured it'd work. I says,
"Remember that Jacob served seven years before
he got to marry Rachel. I'm willing to wait."

That impressed hell out of him, you can bet. He
says, "You truly have the prophetic spirit, Mick.
I have no doubt that someday you'll be Papa in my
place, when the Lord has gathered me unto my
fathers. But I hope you'll also remember that Jacob
married Rachel, but he first married the older
daughter, Leah."

The ugly one, I thought, but I didn't say it. I just
smiled and told him how I'd remember that, and
there was plenty of time to talk about it tomorrow,
because it was dark now and I was tired and a lot
of things had happened to me today that I had to
think over. I was really getting into the spirit of
this Bible thing, and so I says to him, "Remember
that before Jacob could dream of the ladder into
heaven, he had to sleep."

Everybody laughed, but Papa Lem wasn't satisfied yet. He was willing to let the marriage thing
wait for a few days. But there was one thing that
couldn't wait. He looks me in the eye and he says,
"Mick, you got a choice to make. The Lord says
those who aren't for me are against me. Joshua
said choose ye this day whom ye will serve. And
Moses said, 'I call heaven and earth to record this
day against you, that I have set before you life and
death, blessing and cursing: therefore choose life,
that both thou and thy seed may live.' "

Well I don't think you can put it much plainer
than that. I could choose to live there among the
chosen people, surrounded by dirty kids and a

slimy old man telling me who to marry and whether I could raise my own children, or I could choose to leave and get my brains blasted out or maybe just pick up a stiff dose of cancer—I wasn't altogether sure whether they'd do it quick or slow. I kind of figured they'd do it quick, though, so I'd have no chance to spill my seed among the daughters of Esau.

So I gave him my most solemn and hypocritical promise that I would serve the Lord and live among them all the days of my life. Like I told you, I didn't know whether he could tell if I was lying or not. But he nodded and smiled so it looked like he believed me. Trouble was, I knew *he* was lying, and so that meant he *didn't* believe me, and that meant I was in deep poo, as Mr. Kaiser's boy Greggy always said. In fact, he was pretty angry and pretty scared, too, even though he tried to hide it by smiling and keeping a lid on himself. But I knew that he knew that I had no intention of staying there with those crazy people who knocked up their cousins and stayed about as ignorant as I ever saw. Which meant that he was already planning to kill me, and sooner rather than later.

No, I better tell the truth here, cause I wasn't *that* smart. It wasn't till I was halfway to the house that I really wondered if he believed me, and it wasn't till Mama had me with a nice clean pair of pajamas up in a nice clean room, and she was about to take my jeans and shirt and underwear and make *them* nice and clean that it occurred to me that maybe I was going to wish I had more clothes on than pajamas that night. I really got kind of mad before she finally gave me back my clothes—she was scared that if she didn't do what I said, I'd do something to her. And then I got to thinking that maybe I'd made things even *worse* by not giving her the clothes, because that might make them think that I was planning to skip out, and so maybe they weren't planning to kill me before but now they would, and so I probably just made things worse. Except when it came down to it, I'd rather be wrong about the one thing and at least have my clothes, than be wrong about the other thing and have to gallivant all over the country in pajamas. You don't get much mileage on country roads barefoot in pajamas, even in the summer.

As soon as Mama left and went on downstairs, I got dressed again, including my shoes, and climbed in under the covers. I'd slept out in the open, so I didn't mind sleeping in my clothes. What drove me crazy was getting my shoes on the sheets. They would've yelled at me so bad at the Children's Home.

I laid there in the dark, trying to think what I was going to do. I pretty much knew how to get from this house out to the road, but what good would that do me? I didn't know where I was or where the road led or how far to go, and you don't cut cross country in North Carolina—if you don't trip over something in the dark, you'll bump into some moonshine or marijuana operation and they'll blast your head off, not to mention the danger of getting your throat bit out by some tobacco farmer's mean old dog. So there I'd be running along a road that leads nowhere with them on my tail and if they wanted to run me down, I don't think fear of cancer would slow down your average four-wheeler.

I thought about maybe stealing a car, but I don't have the first idea how to hotwire anything. It wasn't one of the skills you pick up at the Children's Home. I knew the idea of it, somewhat, because I'd done some reading on electricity with the books Mr. Kaiser lent me so I could maybe try getting ready for the GED, but there wasn't a chapter in there on how to get a Lincoln running without a key. Didn't know how to drive, either. All the stuff you pick up from your dad or from your friends at school, I just never picked up at all.

Maybe I dozed off, maybe I didn't. But I suddenly noticed that I could see in the dark. Not *see*, of course. Feel the people moving around. Not far off at first, except like a blur, but I could feel the near ones, the other ones in the house. It was cause they was sparky, of course, but as I laid there feeling them drifting here and there, in the rhythms of sleep and dreams, or walking around, I began to realize that I'd been feeling people all along, only I didn't know it. They wasn't sparky, but I always knew where they were, like shadows drifting in the back of your mind, I didn't even know that I knew it, but they were there. It's like when Diz Riddle got him his glasses when he was ten years old and all of a sudden he just went around whooping and yelling about all the stuff he saw. He al-

ways used to see it before, but he didn't rightly
know what half the stuff was. Like pictures on
coins. He knew the coins was bumpy, but he
didn't know they was pictures and writing and
stuff. That's how this was.

I laid there and I could make a map in my brain
where I could see a whole bunch of different people, and the more I tried, the better I could see.
Pretty soon it wasn't just in that house. I could
feel them in other houses, dimmer and fainter. But
in my mind I didn't see no walls so I didn't know
whether somebody was in the kitchen or in the
bathroom, I had to think it out, and it was hard,
it took all my concentration. The only guide I
had was that I could see electric wires when the
current was flowing through them, so wherever a
light was on or a clock was running or something,
I could feel this thin line, really thin, not like the
shadows of people. It wasn't much, but it gave me
some idea of where some of the walls might be.

If I could've just told who was who I might have
made some guesses about what they was doing.
Who was asleep and who was awake. But I
couldn't even tell who was a kid and who was a
grown-up, cause I couldn't see sizes, just brightness. Brightness was the only way I knew who was
close and who was far.

I was pure lucky I got so much sleep during
the day when that guy was giving me a ride from
Roanoke to Eden. Well, that wasn't lucky, I guess,
since I wished I hadn't gone to Eden at all, but at
least having that long nap meant that I had a better
shot at staying awake until things quieted down.

There was a clump of them in the next house. It was hard to sort them out, cause three of them was a lot brighter, so I thought they was closer, and it took a while to realize that it was probably Mama and Daddy and Papa Lem along with some others. Anyway it was a meeting, and it broke up after a while, and all except Papa Lem came over. I didn't know what the meeting was about, but I knew they was scared and mad. Mostly scared. Well, so was I. But I calmed myself down, the way I'd been practicing, so I didn't accidently kill nobody. That kind of practice made it so I could keep myself from getting too lively and sparky, so they'd think I was asleep. They didn't see as clear as I did, too, so that'd help. I thought maybe they'd all come up and get me, but no, they just all waited downstairs while one of them came up, and he didn't come in and get me, neither. All he did was go to the other rooms and wake up whoever was sleeping there and get them downstairs and out of the house.

Well, that scared me worse than ever. That made it plain what they had in mind, all right. Didn't want me giving off sparks and killing somebody close by when they attacked me. Still, when I thought about it, I realized that it was also a good sign. They was scared of me, and rightly so. I could reach farther and strike harder than any of them. And they saw I could throw off what got tossed at me, when I flung back what Papa Lem's daughter tried to do to me. They didn't know how much I could do.

Neither did I.

Finally all the people was out of the house except the ones downstairs. There was others outside the house, maybe watching, maybe not, but I figured I better not try to climb out the window.

Then somebody started walking up the stairs again, alone. There wasn't nobody else to fetch down, so they could only be coming after me. It was just one person, but that didn't do me no good—even one grown man who knows how to use a knife is better off than me. I still don't have my full growth on me, or at least I sure hope I don't, and the only fights I ever got in were slugging matches in the yard. For a minute I wished I'd took kung fu lessons instead of sitting around reading math and science books to make up for dropping out of school so young. A lot of good math and science was going to do me if I was dead.

The worst thing was I couldn't see him. Maybe they just moved all the children out of the house so they wouldn't make noise in the morning and wake me. Maybe they was just being nice. And this guy coming up the stairs might just be checking on me or bringing me clean clothes or something—I couldn't tell. So how could I twist him up, when I didn't know if they was trying to kill me or what? But if he *was* trying to kill me, I'd wish I'd twisted him before he ever came into the room with me.

Well, that was one decision that got made for me. I laid there wondering what to do for so long that he got to the top of the stairs and came to my room and turned the knob and came in.

I tried to breathe slow and regular, like somebody asleep. Tried to keep from getting too sparky. If it was somebody checking on me, they'd go away.

He didn't go away. And he walked soft, too, so as not to wake me up. He was real scared. So scared that I finally knew there was no way he was there to tuck me in and kiss me good night.

So I tried to twist him, to send sparks at him. But I didn't have any sparks to send! I mean I wasn't mad or anything. I'd never tried to kill somebody on purpose before, it was always because I was already mad and I just lost control and it *happened*. Now I'd been calming myself down so much that I couldn't lose control. I had no sparks at all to send, just my normal shining shadow, and he was right there and I didn't have a second to lose so I rolled over. Toward him, which was maybe dumb, cause I might have run into his knife, but I didn't know yet for sure that he had a knife. All I was thinking was that I had to knock him down or push him or something.

The only person I knocked down was me. I bumped him and hit the floor. He also cut my back with the knife. Not much of a cut, he mostly just snagged my shirt, but if I was scared before, I was terrified now cause I knew he had a knife and I knew even more that I didn't. I scrambled back away from him. There was almost no light from the window; it was like being in a big closet, I couldn't see him, he couldn't see me. Except of course that I *could* see him, or at least sense where he was, and now I was giving off sparks like crazy so unless he was weaker than I thought, he could see me too.

Well, he was weaker than I thought. He just kind of drifted, and I could hear him swishing the knife through the air in front of him. He had no idea where I was.

And all the time I was trying to get madder and madder, and it wasn't working. You can't get mad by trying. Maybe an actor can, but I'm no actor. So I was scared and sparking but I couldn't get that pulse to mess him up. The more I thought about it, the calmer I got.

It's like you've been carrying around a machine gun all your life, accidently blasting people you didn't really want to hurt and then the first time you really want to lay into somebody, it jams.

So I stopped trying to get mad. I just sat there realizing I was going to die, that after I finally got myself under control so I didn't kill people all the time anymore, now that I didn't really want to commit suicide, *now* I was going to get wasted. And they didn't even have the guts to come at me openly. Sneaking in the dark to cut my throat while I was asleep. And in the meeting where they decided to do it, my long lost but loving mama and daddy were right there. Heck, my dear sweet daddy was downstairs right now, waiting for this assassin to come down and tell him that I was dead. Would he cry for me then? Boo hoo my sweet little boy's all gone? Mick is in the cold cold ground?

I was mad. As simple as that. Stop thinking

about being mad, and start thinking about the things that if you think about them, they'll make you mad. I was so sparky with fear that when I got mad, too, it was worse than it ever was before, built up worse, you know. Only when I let it fly, it didn't go for the guy up there swishing his knife back and forth in the dark. That pulse of fire in me went right down through the floor and straight to dear old Dad. I could hear him scream. He felt it, just like that. He felt it. And so did I. Because that wasn't what I meant to do. I only met him that day, but he was my *father*, and I did him worse than I ever did anybody before in my life. I didn't plan to do it. You don't plan to kill your father.

All of a sudden I was blinded by light. For a second I thought it was the other kind of light, sparks, them retaliating, twisting me. Then I realized it was my eyes being blinded, and it was the overhead light in the room that was on. The guy with the knife had finally realized that the only reason not to have the light on was so I wouldn't wake up, but now that I was awake he might as well see what he's doing. Lucky for me the light blinded him just as much as it blinded me, or I'd have been poked before I saw what hit me. Instead I had time to scramble on back to the far corner of the room.

I wasn't no hero. But I was seriously thinking about running at him, attacking a guy with a knife. I would have been killed, but I couldn't think of anything else to do.

Then I thought of something else to do. I got

the idea from the way I could feel the electric current in the wires running from the lightswitch through the wall. That was electricity, and the lady in Roanoke called my sparkiness bio-electricity. I ought to be able to do something with it, shouldn't I?

I thought first that maybe I could short-circuit something, but I didn't think I had that much electricity in me. I thought of maybe tapping into the house current to add to my own juice, but then I remembered that connecting up your body to house current is the same thing other folks call *electrocution*. I mean, maybe I can tap into house wiring, but if I was wrong, I'd be real dead.

But I could still do something. There was a table lamp right next to me. I pulled off the shade and threw it at the guy, who was still standing by the door, thinking about what the scream downstairs meant. Then I grabbed the lamp and turned it on, and then smashed the light bulb on the nightstand. Sparks. Then it was out.

I held the lamp in my hand, like a weapon, so he'd think I was going to beat off his knife with the lamp. And if my plan was a bust, I guess that's what I would've done. But while he was looking at me, getting ready to fight me knife against lamp, I kind of let the jagged end of the lamp rest on the bedspread. And then I used my sparkiness, the anger that was still in me. I couldn't fling it at the guy, or well I could have, but it would've been like the bus driver, a six-month case of lung cancer. By the time he died of *that*, I'd be six months worth of dead from multiple stab wounds to the neck and chest.

So I let my sparkiness build up and flow out along my arm, out along the lamp, like I was making my shadow grow. And it worked. The sparks just went right on down the lamp to the tip, and built up and built up, and all the time I was thinking about how Papa Lem was trying to kill me cause I thought his daughter was ugly and how he made me kill my daddy before I even knew him half a day and that charge built *up*.

It built up enough. Sparks started jumping across inside the broken light bulb, right there against the bedspread. Real sparks, the kind I could *see*, not just feel. And in two seconds that bedspread was on fire. *Then* I yanked the lamp so the cord shot right out of the wall, and I threw it at the guy, and while he was dodging I scooped up the bedspread and ran at him. I wasn't sure whether I'd catch on fire or he would, but I figured he'd be too panicked and surprised to think of stabbing me *through* the bedspread, and sure enough he didn't, he dropped the knife and tried to beat off the bedspread. Which he didn't do too good, because I was still pushing it at him. Then he tried to get through the door, but I kicked his ankle with my shoe, and he fell down, still fighting off the blanket.

I got the knife and sliced right across the back of his thigh with it. Geez it was sharp. Or maybe I was so mad and scared that I cut him stronger than I ever thought I could, but it went clear to the bone. He was screaming from the fire and his leg was gushing blood and the fire was catching on the wallpaper and it occurred to me that they couldn't chase me too good if they was trying to put out a real dandy house fire.

It also occurred to me that I couldn't run away too good if I was dead inside that house fire. And thinking of maybe dying in the fire made me realize that the guy was burning to death and I did it to him, something every bit as terrible as cancer, and *I didn't care*, because I'd killed so many people that it was nothing to me now, when a guy like that was trying to kill me, I wasn't even sorry for his pain, cause he wasn't feeling nothing worse than Old Peleg felt, and in fact that even made me feel pretty good, because it was like getting even for Old Peleg's death, even though it was me killed them both. I mean how could I get *even* for Peleg dying by killing somebody else? Okay, maybe it makes sense in a way, cause it was their fault I was in the orphanage instead of growing up here. Or maybe it made sense because this guy deserved to die, and Peleg didn't, so maybe somebody who deserved it had to die a death as bad as Peleg's, or something. I don't know. I sure as hell wasn't thinking about that then. I just knew that I was hearing a guy scream himself to death and I didn't even want to help him or even *try* to help him or nothing. I wasn't enjoying it, either, I wasn't thinking, Burn you sucker! or anything like that, but I knew right then that I wasn't even human, I was just a monster, like I always thought, like in the slasher movies. This was straight from the

slasher movies, somebody burning up and screaming, and there's the monster just standing there in
the flames and he *isn't burning.*

And that's the truth. I wasn't burning. There
was flames all around me, but it kind of shied
back from me, because I was so full of sparks from
hating myself so bad that it was like the flames
couldn't get through to me. I've thought about
that a lot since then. I mean, even that Swedish
scientist doesn't know all about this bio-electrical
stuff. Maybe when I get real sparky it makes it so
other stuff can't hit me. Maybe that's how some
generals in the Civil War used to ride around in
the open—or maybe that was that general in
World War II, I can't remember—and bullets
didn't hit them or anything. Maybe if you're
charged up enough, things just can't *get* to you. I
don't know. I just know that by the time I finally
decided to open the door and actually opened it,
the whole room was burning and the door was
burning and I just opened it and walked through.
Course now I got a bandage on my hand to prove
that I couldn't grab a hot doorknob without hurting myself a little, but I shouldn't've been able to
stay alive in that room and I came out without
even my hair singed.

I started down the hall, not knowing who was
still in the house. I wasn't used to being able to
see people by their sparkiness yet, so I didn't even
think of checking, I just ran down the stairs carrying that bloody knife. But it didn't matter. They
all ran away before I got there, all except Daddy.
He was lying in the middle of the floor in the

living room, doubled up, lying with his head in a pool of vomit and his butt in a pool of blood, shaking like he was dying of cold. I really done him. I really tore him up inside. I don't think he even saw me. But he was my daddy, and even a monster don't leave his daddy for the fire to get him. So I grabbed his arms to try to pull him out.

I forgot how sparky I was, worse than ever. The second I touched him the sparkiness just rushed out of me and all over him. It never went that way before, just completely surrounded him like he was a part of me, like he was completely drowning in my light. It wasn't what I meant to do at all. I just forgot. I was trying to save him and instead I gave him a hit like I never gave nobody before, and I couldn't stand it, I just screamed.

Then I dragged him out. He was all limp, but even if I killed him, even if I turned him to jelly inside, he wasn't going to burn, that's all I could think of, that and how I ought to walk back into that house myself and up the stairs and catch myself on fire and die.

But I didn't do it, as you might guess. There was people yelling Fire! and shouting Stay back! and I knew that I better get out of there. Daddy's body was lying on the grass in front of the house, and I took off around the back. I thought maybe I heard some gunshots, but it could've been popping and cracking of timbers in the fire, I don't know. I just ran around the house and along toward the road, and if there was people in my way they just got *out* of my way, because even the most dimwitted inbred pukebrained kid in that whole village would've seen my sparks, I was so hot.

I ran till the asphalt ended and I was running on the dirt road. There was clouds so the moon was hardly any light at all, and I kept stumbling off the road into the weeds. I fell once and when I was getting up I could see the fire behind me. The whole house was burning, and there was flames above it in the trees. Come to think of it there hadn't been all that much rain, and those trees were dry. A lot more than one house was going to burn tonight, I figured, and for a second I even thought maybe nobody'd chase me.

But that was about as stupid an idea as I ever had. I mean, if they wanted to kill me before because I said Papa Lem's girl was ugly, how do you think they felt about me now that I burned down their little hidden town? Once they realized I was gone, they'd be after me and I'd be lucky if they shot me quick.

I even thought about cutting off the road, dangerous or not, and hiding in the woods. But I decided to get as much distance as I could along the road till I saw headlights.

Just when I decided that, the road ended. Just bushes and trees. I went back, tried to find the road. It must have turned but I didn't know which way. I was tripping along like a blind man in the grass, trying to feel my way to the ruts of the dirt road, and of course that's when I saw headlights away off toward the burning houses—there was at least three houses burning now. They knew the town was a total loss by now, they was probably just leaving enough folks to get all the children out and away to a safe place, while the men came after me. It's what *I* would've done, and to hell with cancer, they knew I couldn't stop them all before they did what they wanted to me. And here I couldn't even find the road to get away from them. By the time their headlights got close enough to show the road, it'd be too late to get away.

I was about to run back into the woods when all of a sudden a pair of headlights went on not twenty feet away, and pointed right at me. I damn near wet my pants. I thought, Mick Winger, you are a dead little boy right this second.

And then I heard her calling to me. "Get on over here, Mick, you idiot, don't stand there in the light, get on over here." It was the lady from Roanoke. I still couldn't see her cause of the lights, but I knew her voice, and I took off. The road didn't end, it just turned a little and she was parked right where the dirt road met up sideways with a gravel road. I got around to the door of the car she was driving, or truck or whatever it was— a four-wheel-drive Blazer maybe, I know it had a four-wheel-drive shift lever in it—anyway the door was locked and she was yelling at me to get *in* and I was yelling back that it was *locked* until finally she unlocked it and I climbed in. She backed up so fast and swung around onto the gravel in a spin that near threw me right out the door, since I hadn't closed it yet. Then she took off so fast going *forward*, spitting gravel behind her, that the door closed itself.

"Fasten your seat belt," she says to me.

"Did you follow me here?" I says.

"No, I just happened to be here picnicking," she says. "Fasten your damn *seat belt*."

I did, but then I turned around in my seat and looked out the back. There was five or six sets of headlights, making the job to get from the dirt road onto the gravel road. We didn't have more than a mile on them.

"We've been looking for this place for years," she says. "We thought it was in Rockingham County, that's how far off we were."

"Where is it, then?" I says.

"Alamance County," she says.

And then I says, "I don't give a damn what county it is! I killed my own daddy back there!"

And she says to me, "Don't get mad now, don't get mad at me, I'm sorry, just calm down." That was all she could think of, how I might get mad and lose control and kill her, and I don't blame her, cause it was the hardest thing I ever did, keeping myself from busting out right there in the car, and it would've killed her, too. The pain in my hand was starting to get to me, too, from where I grabbed the doorknob. It was just building up and building up.

She was driving a lot faster than the headlights reached. We'd be going way too fast for a curve before she even saw it, and then she'd slam on the brakes and we'd skid and sometimes I couldn't believe we didn't just roll over and crash. But she always got out of it.

I couldn't face back anymore. I just sat there with my eyes closed, trying to get calm, and then I'd remember my daddy who I didn't even *like* but he was my daddy lying there in his blood and his puke, and I'd remember that guy who burned to death up in my room and even though I didn't care at the time, I sure cared now, I was so angry and scared and I hated myself so bad I couldn't hold it in, only I also couldn't let it out, and I kept wishing I could just die. Then I realized that the guys following us were close enough that I could feel them. Or no it wasn't that they was close. They was just so *mad* that I could see their sparks flying like never before. Well as long as I could see them I could let fly, couldn't I? I just flung out toward them. I don't know if I hit them. I don't know if my bio-electricity is something I can throw like that or what. But at least I shucked it off myself, and I didn't mess up the lady who was driving.

When we hit asphalt again, I found out that I didn't know what crazy driving was before. She peeled out and now she began to look at a curve ahead and then switch off the headlights until she was halfway through the curve, it was the craziest thing I ever saw, but it also made sense. They had to be following our lights, and when our lights went out they wouldn't know where we was for a minute. They also wouldn't know that the road curved ahead, and they might even crash up or at least they'd have to slow down. Of course, we had a real good chance of ending up eating trees ourselves, but she drove like she knew what she was doing.

We came to a straight section with a crossroads about a mile up. She switched off the lights again, and I thought maybe she was going to turn, but she didn't. Just went on and on and on, straight into the pitch black. Now, that straight section was long, but it didn't go on forever, and I don't care how good a driver you are, you can't keep track of how far you've gone in the dark. Just when I thought for sure we'd smash into something, she let off the gas and reached her hand out the window with a flashlight. We was still going pretty fast, but the flashlight was enough to make a reflector up ahead flash back at us, so she knew where the curve was, and it was farther off than I thought. She whipped us around that curve and then around another, using just a couple of blinks from the flashlight, before she switched on her headlights again.

I looked behind us to see if I could see anybody. "You lost them!" I says.

"Maybe," she says. "You tell *me*."

So I tried to feel where they might be, and sure enough, they was sparky enough that I could just barely tell where they was, away back. Split up, smeared out. "They're going every which way," I says.

"So we lost a few of them," she says. "They aren't going to give up, you know."

"I know," I says.

"You're the hottest thing going," she says.

"And you're a daughter of Esau," I says.

"Like hell I am," she says. "I'm a great-great-great-granddaughter of Jacob Yow, who happened to be bio-electrically talented. Like if you're tall and athletic, you can play basketball. That's all it is, just a natural talent. Only he went crazy and started inbreeding his whole family, and they've got these stupid ideas about being the chosen of God and all the time they're just *murderers*."

"Tell me about it," I says.

"You can't help it," she says. "You didn't have anybody to teach you. I'm not blaming you."

But I was blaming me.

She says, "Ignorant, that's what they are. Well, my grandpa didn't want to just keep reading the Bible and killing any revenuers or sheriffs or whatever who gave us trouble. He wanted to find out what we *are*. He also didn't want to marry the slut they picked out for him because he wasn't particularly dusty. So he left. They hunted him down and tried to kill him, but he got away, and he married. And he also studied and became a doctor and his kids grew up knowing that they had to find out what it *is*, this power. It's like the old stories of witches, women who get mad and suddenly your cows start dying. Maybe they didn't even know they were doing it. Summonings and love spells and come-hithers, everybody can do it a little, just like everybody can throw a ball and sometimes make a basket, but some people can do it better than others. And Papa Lem's people, they do it best of all, better and better, because they're breeding for it. We've got to stop them, don't you see? We've got to keep them from learning how to control it. Because now we know more about it. It's all tied up with the way the human body heals itself. In Sweden they've been changing the currents around to heal tumors. Cancer. The opposite of what you've been doing, but it's the same principle. Do you know what that means? If they could control it, Lem's people could be healers, not killers. Maybe all it takes is to do it with love, not anger."

"Did you kill them little girls in orphanages with love?" I says.

And she just drives, she doesn't say a thing, just drives. "Damn," she says, "it's raining."

The road was slick in two seconds. She slowed way down. It came down harder and harder. I looked behind us and there was headlights back there again. Way back, but I could still see them. "They're on us again," I says.

"I can't go any faster in the rain," she says.

"It's raining on them too," I says.

"Not with my luck."

And I says, "It'll put the fire out. Back where they live."

And she says, "It doesn't matter. They'll move. They know we found them, because we picked you up. So they'll move."

I apologized for causing trouble, and she says, "We couldn't let you die in there. I had to go there and save you if I could."

"Why?" I ask her. "Why not let me die?"

"Let me put it another way," she says. "If you decided to stay with them, I had to go in there and kill you."

And I says to her, "You're the queen of compassion, you know?" And I thought about it a little. "You're just like they are, you know?" I says. "You wanted to get pregnant just like they did. You wanted to breed me like a stud horse."

"If I wanted to *breed* you," she says, "I would have done it on the hill this morning. Yesterday morning. You would've done it. And I should've made you, because if you went with them, our only hope was to have a child of yours that we could raise to be a decent person. Only it turned out you're a decent person, so we didn't have to kill you. Now we can study you and learn about this from the strongest living example of the phenomenon"—I don't know how to pronounce that, but you know what I mean. Or what she meant, anyway.

And I says to her, "Maybe I don't want you to study me, did you think of that?"

And she says to me, "Maybe what you want don't amount to a goldfish fart." Or anyway that's what she meant.

That's about when they started shooting at us. Rain or no rain, they was pushing it so they got close enough to shoot, and they wasn't half bad at it, seeing as the first bullet we knew about went right through the back window and in between us and smacked a hole in the windshield. Which made all kinds of cracks in the glass so she couldn't see, which made her slow down more, which meant they was even closer.

Just then we whipped around a corner and our headlights lit up a bunch of guys getting out of a car with guns in their hands, and she says, "Finally." So I figured they was some of her people, there to take the heat off. But at that same second Lem's people must have shot out a tire or maybe she just got a little careless for a second cause after all she couldn't see too good through the windshield, but anyway she lost control and we skidded and flipped over, rolled over it felt like five times, all in slow motion, rolling and rolling, the doors popping open and breaking off, the windshield cracking and crumbling away, and there we hung in our seat belts, not talking or nothing, except maybe I was saying O my God or something and then we smacked into something and just stopped, which jerked us around inside the car and then it was all over.

I heard water rushing. A stream, I thought. We can wash up. Only it wasn't a stream, it was the gasoline pouring out of the tank. And then I heard gunshots from back up by the road. I didn't know who was fighting who, but if the wrong guys won they'd just love to catch us in a nice hot gasoline fire. Getting out wasn't going to be all that hard. The doors were gone so we didn't have to climb out a window or anything.

We were leaned over on the left side, so her door was mashed against the ground. I says to her, "We got to climb out my door." I had brains enough to hook one arm up over the lip of the car before I unbuckled my seat belt, and then I hoisted myself out and stayed perched up there on the side of the car, up in the air, so I could reach down and help her out.

Only she wasn't climbing out. I yelled at her and she didn't answer. I thought for a second she was dead, but then I saw that her sparks was still there. Funny, how I never saw she had any sparkiness before, because I didn't know to look for it, but now, even though it was dim, I could see it. Only it wasn't so dim, it was real busy, like she was trying to heal herself. The gurgling was still going on, and everything smelled like gasoline. There was still shooting going on. And even if nobody came down to start us on fire on purpose, I saw enough car crashes at the movies to know you didn't need a match to start a car on fire. I sure didn't want to be near the car if it caught, and I sure didn't want her *in* it. But I couldn't see how to climb down in and pull her out. I mean I'm not a weakling but I'm not Mr. Universe either.

It felt like I sat there for a whole minute before I realized I didn't have to pull her out my side of the car, I could pull her out the *front* cause the whole windshield was missing and the roof was only mashed down a little, cause there was a roll-bar in the car—that was real smart, putting a roll-bar in. I jumped off the car. It wasn't raining right here, but it *had* rained, so it was slippery and wet. Or maybe it was slippery from the gasoline, I don't know. I got around the front of the car and up to the windshield, and I scraped the bits of glass off with my shoe. Then I crawled partway in and reached under her and undid her seat belt, and tried to pull her out, but her legs was hung up under the steering wheel and it took forever, it was terrible, and all the time I kept listening for her to breathe, and she didn't breathe, and so I kept getting more scared and frustrated and all I was thinking about was how she had to live, she couldn't be dead, she just got through saving my life and now she was dead and she couldn't be and I was going to get her out of the car even if I had to break her legs to do it, only I didn't have to break her legs and she finally slid out and I dragged her away from the car. It didn't catch on fire, but I couldn't know it wasn't going to.

And anyway all I cared about then was her, not breathing, lying there limp on the grass with her neck all floppy and I was holding on to her crying and angry and scared and I had us both covered with sparks, like we was the same person, just completely covered, and I was crying and saying, Live! I couldn't even call her by name or nothing because I didn't know her name. I just know that I was shaking like I had the chills and so was she and she was breathing now and whimpering like somebody just stepped on a puppy and the sparks just kept flowing around us both and I felt like somebody sucked everything out of me, like I was a wet towel and somebody wrung me out and flipped me into a corner, and then I don't remember until I woke up here.

What did it feel like? What you did to her?

It felt like when I covered her with light, it was like I was taking over doing what her own body should've done, it was like I was healing her. Maybe I got that idea because she said something about healing when she was driving the car, but she wasn't breathing when I dragged her out, and then she was breathing. So I want to know if I healed her. Because if she got healed when I covered her with my own light, then maybe I didn't kill my daddy either, because it was kind of like that, I *think* it was kind of like that, what happened when I dragged him out of the house.

I been talking a long time now, and you still told me nothing. Even if you think I'm just a killer and you want me dead, you can tell me about her. Is she alive?

Yes.

Well then how come I can't see her? How come she isn't here with the rest of you?

She had some surgery. It takes time to heal.

But did I help her? Or did I twist her? You got to tell me. Cause if I didn't help her then I hope I fail your test and you kill me cause I can't think of a good reason why I should be alive if all I can do is kill people.

You helped her, Mick. That last bullet caught her in the head. That's why she crashed.

But she wasn't bleeding!

It was dark, Mick. You couldn't see. You had her blood all over you. But it doesn't matter now. We have the bullet out. As far as we can tell, there was no brain damage. There should have been. She should have been dead.

So I did help her.

Yes. But we don't know how. All kinds of stories, you know, about faith healing, that sort of thing. Laying on of hands. Maybe it's the kind of thing you did, merging the bio-magnetic field. A lot of things don't make any sense yet. There's no

way we can see that the tiny amount of electricity in a human bio-electric system could influence somebody a hundred miles off, but they summoned you, and you came. We need to study you, Mick. We've never had anybody as powerful as you. Tell the truth, maybe there's never been anybody like you. Or maybe all the healings in the New Testament—

I don't want to hear about no testaments. Papa Lem gave me about all the testaments I ever need to hear about.

Will you help us, Mick?

Help you how?

Let us study you.

Go ahead and study.

Maybe it won't be enough just to study how you *heal* people.

I'm not going to kill nobody for you. If you try to make me kill somebody I'll kill you first till you have to kill me just to save your own lives, do you understand me?

Calm down, Mick. Don't get angry. There's plenty of time to think about things. Actually we're glad that you don't want to kill anybody. If you enjoyed it, or even if you hadn't been able to control it and kept on indiscriminately killing anyone who enraged you, you wouldn't have lived to be seventeen. Because yes, we're scientists, or at least we're finally learning enough that we can start being scientists. But first we're human beings, and we're in the middle of a war, and children like you are the weapons. If they ever got someone like you to stay with them, work with them, you

could seek us out and destroy us. That's what they wanted you to do.

That's right, that's one thing Papa Lem said, I don't know if I mentioned it before, but he said that the children of Israel were supposed to kill every man, woman, and child in Canaan, cause idolaters had to make way for the children of God.

Well, you see, that's why our branch of the family left. We didn't think it was such a terrific idea, wiping out the entire human race and replacing it with a bunch of murderous, incestuous religious fanatics. For the last twenty years, we've been able to keep them from getting somebody like you, because we've murdered the children that were so powerful they had to put them outside to be reared by others.

Except me.

It's a war. We didn't like killing children. But it's like bombing the place where your enemies are building a secret weapon. The lives of a few children—no, that's a lie. It nearly split us apart ourselves, the arguments over that. Letting you live—it was a terrible risk. I voted against it every time. And I don't apologize for that, Mick. Now that you know what they are, and you chose to leave, I'm glad I lost. But so many things could have gone wrong.

They won't put any more babies out to orphanages now, though. They're not that dumb.

But now we have *you*. Maybe we can learn how to block what they do. Or how to heal the people they attack. Or how to identify sparkiness, as you call it, from a distance. All kinds of possibilities.

But sometime in the future, Mick, you may be the only weapon we have. Do you understand that?

I don't want to.

I know.

You wanted to kill me?

I wanted to protect people from you. It was safest. Mick, I really am glad it worked out this way.

I don't know whether to believe you, Mr. Kaiser. You're such a good liar. I thought you were so nice to me all that time because you were just a nice guy.

Oh, he is, Mick. He's a nice guy. Also a damn fine liar. We kind of needed both those attributes in the person we had looking out for you.

Well, anyway, that's over with.

What's over with?

Killing me. Isn't it?

That's up to you, Mick. If you ever start getting crazy on us, or killing people that aren't part of this war of ours—

I won't do that!

But if you did, Mick. It's never too late to kill you.

Can I see her?

See who?

The lady from Roanoke! Isn't it about time you told me her name?

Come on. She can tell you herself.

St. Amy's Tale

MOTHER COULD KILL with her hands. Father could fly. These are miracles. But they were not miracles then. Mother Elouise taught me that there were no miracles then.

I am the child of Wreckers, born while the angel was in them. This is why I am called Saint Amy, though I perceive nothing in me that should make me holier than any other old woman. Yet Mother Elouise denied the angel in her, too, and it was no less there.

Sift your fingers through the soil, all you who read my words. Take your spades of iron and your picks of stone. Dig deep. You will find no ancient works of man hidden there. For the Wreckers passed through the world, and all the vanity was

consumed in fire; all the pride broke in pieces
when it was smitten by God's shining hand.

Elouise leaned on the rim of the computer key-
board. All around her the machinery was alive,
the screens displaying information. Elouise felt
nothing but weariness. She was leaning because,
for a moment, she had felt a frightening vertigo. As
if the world underneath the airplane had dissolved
and slipped away into a rapidly receding star and
she would never be able to land.

True enough, she thought. *I'll never be able to
land, not in the world I knew.*

"Getting sentimental about the old computers?"

Elouise, startled, turned in her chair and faced
her husband, Charlie. At that moment the airplane lurched, but like sailors accustomed to the
shifting of the sea, they adjusted unconsciously
and did not notice the imbalance.

"Is it noon already?" she asked.

"It's the mortal equivalent of noon. I'm too tired
to fly this thing anymore, and it's a good thing
Bill's at the controls."

"Hungry?"

Charlie shook his head. "But Amy probably is,"
he said.

"Voyeur," said Elouise.

Charlie liked to watch Elouise nurse their
daughter. But despite her accusation, Elouise
knew there was nothing sexual in it. Charlie liked
the idea of Elouise being Amy's mother. He liked

the way Amy's sucking resembled the sucking of
a calf or a lamb or a puppy. He had said, "It's the
best thing we kept from the animals. The best
thing we didn't throw away."

"Better than sex?" Elouise had asked. And Charlie had only smiled.

Amy was playing with a rag doll in the only
large clear space in the airplane, near the exit door.
"Mommy Mommy Mamommy Mommy-o," Amy
said. The child stood and reached to be picked up.
Then she saw Charlie. "Daddy Addy Addy."

"Hi," Charlie said.

"Hi," Amy answered. "Ha-ee." She had only
just learned to close the diphthong, and she exag-
gerated it. Amy played with the buttons on Elouise's shirt, trying to undo them.

"Greedy," Elouise said, laughing.

Charlie unbuttoned the shirt for her, and Amy
seized on the nipple after only one false grab. She
sucked noisily, tapping her hand gently against
Elouise's breast as she ate.

"I'm glad we're so near finished," Elouise said.
"She's too old to be nursing now."

"That's right. Throw the little bird out of the
nest."

"Go to bed," Elouise said.

Amy recognized the phrase. She pulled away.
"La-lo," she said.

"That's right. Daddy's going to sleep," Elouise
said.

Elouise watched as Charlie stripped off most of
his clothing and lay down on the pad. He smiled

once, then turned over, and was immediately
asleep. He was in tune with his body. Elouise
knew that he would awaken in exactly six hours,
when it was time for him to take the controls
again.

Amy's sucking was a subtle pleasure now,
though it had been agonizing the first few months,
and painful again when Amy's first teeth had
come in and she had learned to her delight that by
nipping she could make her mother scream. But
better to nurse her than ever have her eat the predi-
gested pap that was served as food on the airplane.
Elouise thought wryly that it was even worse than
the microwaved veal cordon bleu that they used
to inflict on commercial passengers. Only eight
years ago. And they had calibrated their fuel so
exactly that when they took the last draft of fuel
from the last of their storage tanks, the tank registered empty; they would burn the last of the pro-
cessed petroleum, instead of putting it back into
the earth. All their caches were gone now, and
they would be at the tender mercies of the world
that they themselves had created.

Still, there was work to do; the final work, in
the final checks. Elouise held Amy with one arm
while she used her free hand slowly to key in the
last program that her role as commander required
her to use. Elouise Private, she typed. Teacher
teacher I declare I see someone's underwear, she
typed. On the screen appeared the warning she
had put there: "You may think you're lucky finding this program, but unless you know the magic

words, an alarm is going to go off all over this airplane and you'll be had. No way out of it, sucker. Love, Elouise."

Elouise, of course, knew the magic words. Einstein sucks, she typed. The screen went blank, and the alarm did not go off.

Malfunction? she queried. "None," answered the computer.

Tamper? she queried, and the computer answered, "None."

Nonreport? she queried, and the computer flashed, "AFscanP7bb55."

Elouise had not really been dozing. But still she was startled, and she lurched forward, disturbing Amy, who really had fallen asleep. "No no no," said Amy, and Elouise forced herself to be patient; she soothed her daughter back to sleep before pursuing whatever it was that her guardian program had caught. Whatever it was? Oh, she knew what it was. It was treachery. The one thing she had been sure *her* group, *her* airplane would never have. Other groups of Rectifiers—wreckers, they called themselves, having adopted their enemies' name for them—other groups had had their spies or their fainthearts, but not Bill or Heather or Ugly-Bugly.

Specify, she typed.

The computer was specific.

Over northern Virginia, as the airplane followed its careful route to find and destroy everything made of metal, glass, and plastic; somewhere over northern Virginia, the airplane's path bent slightly to the south, and on the return, at the same place, the airplane's path bent slightly to the north, so that a strip of northern Virginia two kilometers long and a few dozen meters wide could contain some nonbiodegradable artifact, hidden from the airplane, and if Elouise had not queried this program, she would never have known it.

But she should have known it. When the plane's course bent, alarms should have sounded. Someone had penetrated the first line of defense. But Bill could not have done that, nor could Heather, really—they didn't have the sophistication to break up a bubble program. Ugly-Bugly?

She knew it wasn't faithful old Ugly-Bugly. No, not her.

The computer voluntarily flashed, "Override M577b, commandmo4, intwis CtTttT." It was an apology. Someone aboard ship had found the alarm override program and the overrides for the alarm overrides. Not my fault, the computer was saying.

Elouise hesitated for a moment. She looked down at her daughter and moved a curl of red hair away from Amy's eye. Elouise's hand trembled. But she was a woman of ice, yes, all frozen where compassion made other women warm. She prided herself on that, on having frozen the last warm places in her—frozen so goddamn rigid that it was only a moment's hesitation. And then she reached out and asked for the access code used to perform the treachery, asked for the name of the traitor.

The computer was even less compassionate than Elouise. It hesitated not at all.

The computer did not underline; the letters on the screen were no larger than normal. Yet Elouise felt the words as a shout, and she answered them silently with a scream.

Charles Evan Hardy, b24ag61-richlandWA.

It was Charlie who was the traitor—Charlie, her sweet, soft, hard-bodied husband, Charlie who secretly was trying to undo the end of the world.

God has destroyed the world before. Once in a flood, when Noah rode it out in the Ark. And once the tower of the world's pride was destroyed in the confusion of tongues. The other times, if there were any other times, those times are all forgotten.

The world will probably be destroyed again, unless we repent. And don't think you can hide from the angels. They start out as ordinary people, and you never know which ones. Suddenly God puts the power of destruction in their hands, and they destroy. And just as suddenly, when all the destruction is done, the angel leaves them, and they're ordinary people. Just my mother and my father.

I can't remember Father Charlie's face. I was too young.

Mother Elouise told me often about Father Charlie. He was born far to the west in a land where water only comes to the crops in ditches, almost never from the sky. It was a land unblessed by God. Men lived there, they believed, only by the strength of their own hands. Men made their ditches and forgot about God and became scientists. Father Charlie became a scientist. He worked on tiny animals, breaking their heart of hearts and combining it in new ways. Hearts were broken too often where he worked, and one of the little animals escaped and killed people until they lay in great heaps like fish in the ship's hold.

But this was not the destruction of the world.

Oh, they were giants in those days, and they forgot the Lord, but when their people lay in piles of moldering flesh and brittling bone, they remembered they were weak.

Mother Elouise said, "Charlie came weeping." This is how Father Charlie became an angel. He saw what the giants had done, by thinking they were greater than God. At first he sinned in his grief. Once he cut his own throat. They put Mother Elouise's blood in him to save his life. This is how they met: In the forest where he had gone to die privately, Father Charlie woke up from a sleep he thought would be forever to see a woman lying next to him in the tent and a doctor bending over them both. When he saw that this woman gave her blood to him whole and unstintingly, he forgot his wish to die. He loved her forever. Mother Elouise said he loved her right up to the day she killed him.

When they were finished, they had a sort of ceremony, a sort of party. "A benediction," said Bill, solemnly sipping at the gin. "Amen and amen."

"My shift," Charlie said, stepping into the cockpit. Then he noticed that everyone was there and that they were drinking the last of the gin, the bottle that had been saved for the end. "Well, happy us," Charlie said, smiling.

Bill got up from the controls of the 787. "Any preferences on where we set down?" he asked. Charlie took his place.

The others looked at one another. Ugly-Bugly shrugged. "God, who ever thought about it?"

"Come on, we're all futurists," Heather said. "You must know where you want to live."

"Two thousand years from now," Ugly-Bugly said. "I want to live in the world the way it'll be two thousand years from now."

"Ugly-Bugly opts for resurrection," Bill said. "I, however, long for the bosom of Abraham."

"Virginia," said Elouise. They turned to face her. Heather laughed.

"Resurrection," Bill intoned, "the bosom of Abraham, and Virginia. You have no poetry, Elouise."

"I've written down the coordinates of the place where we are supposed to land," Elouise said. She handed them to Charlie. He did not avoid her gaze. She watched him read the paper. He showed no sign of recognition. For a moment she hoped that it had all been a mistake, but no. She would not let herself be misled by her desires.

"Why Virginia?" Heather asked.

Charlie looked up. "It's central."

"It's east coast," Heather said.

"It's central in the high survival area. There isn't much of a living to be had in the western mountains or on the plains. It's not so far south as to be in hunter-gatherer country and not so far north as to be unsurvivable for a high proportion of the people. Barring a hard winter."

"All very good reasons," Elouise said. "Fly us there, Charlie."

Did his hands tremble as he touched the controls? Elouise watched very carefully, but he did not tremble. Indeed, he was the only one who did not. Ugly-Bugly suddenly began to cry, tears coming from her good eye and streaming down her good cheek. *Thank God she doesn't cry out of the other side,* Elouise thought; then she was angry at herself, for she had thought Ugly-Bugly's deformed face didn't bother her anymore. Elouise was angry at herself, but it only made her cold inside, determined that there would be no failure. Her mission would be complete. No allowances made for personal cost.

Elouise suddenly started out of her contemplative mood to find that the two other women had left the cockpit—their sleep shift, though it was doubtful they would sleep. Charlie silently flew the plane, while Bill sat in the copilot's seat, pouring himself the last drop from the bottle. He was looking at Elouise.

"Cheers," Elouise said to him.

He smiled sadly back at her. "Amen," he said. Then he leaned back and sang softly:

Praise God, from whom all blessings flow.
Praise him, ye creatures here below.
Praise him, who slew the wicked host.
Praise Father, Son, and Holy Ghost.

Then he reached for Elouise's hand. She was surprised, but let him take it. He bent to her and kissed her palm tenderly. "For many have entertained angels unaware," he said to her.

A few moments later he was asleep. Charlie and Elouise sat in silence. The plane flew on south as darkness overtook them from the east. At first their silence was almost affectionate. But as Elouise sat and sat, saying nothing, she felt the silence grow cold and terrible, and for the first time she realized that when the airplane landed, Charlie would be her—Charlie, who had been half her life for these last few years, whom she had never lied to and who had never lied to her—would be her enemy.

I have watched the little children do a dance called Charlie-El. They sing a little song to it, and if I remember the words, it goes like this:

> *I am made of bones and glass.*
> *Let me pass, let me pass.*
> *I am made of brick and steel.*
> *Take my heel, take my heel.*
> *I was killed just yesterday.*
> *Kneel and pray, kneel and pray.*
> *Dig a hole where I can sleep.*
> *Dig it deep, dig it deep.*
> *Will I go to heaven or hell?*
> *Charlie-El. Charlie-El.*

I think they are already nonsense words to the children. But the poem first got passed word of mouth around Richmond when I was little, and living in Father Michael's house. The children do not try to answer their song. They just sing it and do a very clever little dance while they sing. They always end the song with all the children falling down on the ground, laughing. That is the best way for the song to end.

Charlie brought the airplane straight down into a field, great hot winds pushing against the ground as if to shove it back from the plane. The field caught fire, but when the plane had settled upon its three wheels, foam streaked out from the belly of the machine and overtook the flames. Elouise watched from the cockpit, thinking, *Wherever the foam has touched, nothing will grow for years.* It seemed symmetrical to her. Even in the last moments of the last machine, it must poison the earth. Elouise held Amy on her lap and thought of trying to explain it to the child. But Elouise knew Amy would not understand or remember.

"Last one dressed is a sissy-wissy," said Ugly-Bugly in her husky, ancient-sounding voice. They had dressed and undressed in front of each other for years now, but today as the old plastic-polluted clothing came off and the homespun went on, they felt and acted like school kids on their first day in coed gym. Amy caught the spirit of it and kept yelling at the top of her lungs. No one thought to quiet her. There was no need. This was a celebration.

But Elouise, long accustomed to self-examination, forced herself to realize that there was a strain to her frolicking. She did not believe it, not really. Today was not a happy day, and it was not just from knowing the confrontation that lay ahead. There was something so final about the death of the last of the engines of mankind. Surely something could be—but she forced the thought from her, forced the coldness in her to overtake that sentiment. Surely she could not be seduced by the beauty of the airplane. Surely she must remember that it was not the machines but what they inevitably did to mankind that was evil.

They looked and felt a little awkward, almost silly, as they left the plane and stood around in the blackened field. They had not yet lost their feel for stylish clothing, and the homespun was so lumpy and awkward and rough. It didn't look right on any of them.

Amy clung to her doll, awed by the strange scenery. In her life she had been out of the airplane only once, and that was when she was an infant. She watched as the trees moved unpredictably. She winced at the wind in her eyes. She touched her cheek, where her hair moved back and forth in the breeze, and hunted through her vocabulary for a word to name the strange invisible touch on her skin. "Mommy," she said. "Uh! Uh! Uh!"

Elouise understood. "Wind," she said. The sounds were still too hard for Amy, and the child did not attempt to say the word. *Wind*, thought Elouise, and immediately thought of Charlie. Her best memory of Charlie was in the wind. It was during his death-wish time, not long after his suicide attempt. He had insisted on climbing a mountain, and she knew that he meant to fall. So she had climbed with him, even though there was a storm coming up. Charlie was angry all the way. She remembered a terrible hour clinging to the face of a cliff, held only by small bits of metal forced into cracks in the rock. She had insisted on remaining tied to Charlie. "If one of us fell, it would only drag the other down, too," he kept saying. "I know," she kept answering. And so Charlie had not fallen, and they made love for the first time in a shallow cave, with the wind howling outside and occasional sprays of rain coming in to dampen them. They refused to be dampened. Wind. Damn.

And Elouise felt herself go cold and unemotional, and they stood on the edge of the field in the shade of the first trees. Elouise had left the Rectifier near the plane, set on 360 degrees. In a few minutes the Rectifier would go off, and they had to watch, to witness the end of their work.

Suddenly Bill shouted, laughed, held up his wrist. "My watch!" he cried.

"Hurry," Charlie said. "There's time."

Bill unbuckled his watch and ran toward the Rectifier. He tossed the watch. It landed within a few meters of the small machine. Then Bill returned to the group, jogging and shaking his head. "Jesus, what a moron! Three years wiping out everything east of the Mississippi, and I almost save a digital chronograph."

"Dixie Instruments?" Heather asked.

"Yeah."

"That's not high technology," she said, and they all laughed. Then they fell silent, and Elouise wondered whether they were all thinking the same thing: that jokes about brand names would be dead within a generation, if they were not already dead. They watched the Rectifier in silence, waiting for the timer to finish its delay. Suddenly there was a shining in the air, a dazzling not-light that made them squint. They had seen this many times before, from the air and from the ground, but this was the last time, and so they saw it as if it were the first.

The airplane corroded as if a thousand years were passing in seconds. But it wasn't a true corrosion. There was no rust—only dissolution as molecules separated and seeped down into the loosened earth. Glass became sand; plastic corrupted to oil; the metal also drifted down into the ground and came to rest in a vein at the bottom of the Rectifier field. Whatever else the metal might look like to a future geologist, it wouldn't look like an artifact. It would look like iron. And with so many similar pockets of iron and copper and aluminum and tin spread all over the once-civilized world, it was not likely that they would suspect human interference. Elouise was amused, thinking of the treatises that would someday be written, about the two states of workable metals—the ore state and the pure-metal vein. She hoped it would retard their progress a little.

The airplane shivered into nothing, and the Rectifier also died in the field. A few minutes after the Rectifier disappeared, the field also faded.

"Amen and amen," said Bill, maudlin again. "All clean now."

Elouise only smiled. She said nothing of the

other Rectifier, which was in her knapsack. Let the others think all the work was done.

Amy poked her finger in Charlie's eye. Charlie swore and set her down. Amy started to cry, and Charlie knelt by her and hugged her. Amy's arms went tightly around his neck. "Give Daddy a kiss," Elouise said.

"Well, time to go," Ugly-Bugly's voice rasped. "Why the hell did you pick this particular spot?"

Elouise cocked her head. "Ask Charlie."

Charlie flushed. Elouise watched him grimly. "Elouise and I once came here," he said. "Before Rectification began. Nostalgia, you know." He smiled shyly, and the others laughed. Except Elouise. She was helping Amy to urinate. She felt the weight of the small Rectifier in her knapsack and did not tell anyone the truth: that she had never been in Virginia before in her life.

"Good a spot as any," Heather said. "Well, bye."

Well, bye. That was all, that was the end of it, and Heather walked away to the west, toward the Shenandoah Valley.

"See ya," Bill said.

"Like hell," Ugly-Bugly added.

Impulsively Ugly-Bugly hugged Elouise, and Bill cried, and then they took off northeast, toward the Potomac, where they would doubtlessly find a community growing up along the clean and fish-filled river.

Just Charlie, Amy, and Elouise left in the empty, blackened field where the airplane had died. Elouise tried to feel some great pain at the separation from the others, but she could not. They had been together every day for years now, going from supply dump to supply dump, wrecking cities and towns, destroying and using up the artificial world. But had they been friends? If it had not been for their task, they would never have been friends. They were not the same kind of people.

And then Elouise was ashamed of her feelings. Not her kind of people? Because Heather liked what grass did to her and had never owned a car or had a driver's license in her life? Because Ugly-Bugly had a face hideously deformed by cancer surgery? Because Bill always worked Jesus into the conversation, even though half the time he was an atheist? Because they just weren't in the same social circles? There were no social circles now. Just people trying to survive in a bitter world they weren't bred for. There were only two classes now: those who would make it and those who wouldn't.

Which class am I? thought Elouise.

"Where should we go?" Charlie asked.

Elouise picked Amy up and handed her to Charlie. "Where's the capsule, Charlie?"

Charlie took Amy and said, "Hey, Amy, baby, I'll bet we find some farming community between here and the Rappahannock."

"Doesn't matter if you tell me, Charlie. The instruments found it before we landed. You did a damn good job on the computer program." She didn't have to say, Not good enough.

Charlie only smiled crookedly. "Here I was hoping you were forgetful." He reached out to touch her knapsack. She pulled abruptly away. He lost his smile. "Don't you know me?" he asked softly.

He would never try to take the Rectifier from her by force. But still. This was the last of the artifacts they were talking about. Was anyone really predictable at such a time? Elouise was not sure. She had thought she knew him well before, yet the time capsule existed to prove that her understanding of Charlie was far from complete.

"I know you, Charlie," she said, "but not as well as I thought. Does it matter? Don't try to stop me."

"I hope you're not too angry," he said.

Elouise couldn't think of anything to say to that. *Anyone could be fooled by a traitor, but only I am fool enough to marry one.* She turned from him and walked into the forest. He took Amy and followed.

All the way through the underbrush Elouise kept expecting him to say something. A threat, for instance: You'll have to kill me to destroy that time capsule. Or a plea: You have to leave it, Elouise, please, please. Or reason, or argument, or anger, or something.

But instead it was just his silent footfalls behind her. Just his occasional playtalk with Amy. Just his singing as he put Amy to sleep on his shoulder.

The capsule had been hidden well. There was no surface sign that men had ever been here. Yet, from the Rectifier's emphatic response, it was obvious that the time capsule was quite large. There must have been heavy, earthmoving equipment. Or was it all done by hand?

"When did you ever find the time?" Elouise asked when they reached the spot.

"Long lunch hours," he said.

She set down her knapsack and then stood there, looking at him.

Like a condemned man who insists on keeping his composure, Charlie smiled wryly and said, "Get on with it, please."

After Father Charlie died, Mother Elouise brought me here to Richmond. She didn't tell anyone that she was a Wrecker. The angel had already left her, and she wanted to blend into the town, be an ordinary person in the world she and her fellow angels had created.

Yet she was incapable of blending in. Once the angel touches you, you cannot go back, even when the angel's work is done. She first attracted attention by talking against the stockade. There was once a stockade around the town of Richmond, when there were only a thousand people here. The reason was simple: People still weren't used to the hard way life was without the old machines. They had not yet learned to depend on the miracle of Christ. They still trusted in their hands, yet their hands could work no more magic. So there were tribes in the winter that didn't know how to find game, that had no reserves of grain, that had no shelter adequate to hold the head of a fire.

"Bring them all in," said Mother Elouise. "There's room for all. There's food for all. Teach them how to build ships and make tools and sail and farm, and we'll all be richer for it."

But Father Michael and Uncle Avram knew more than Mother Elouise. Father Michael had been a Catholic priest before the destruction, and Uncle Avram had been a professor at a university. They had been nobody. But when the angels of destruction finished their work, the angels of life began to work in the hearts of men. Father Michael threw off his old allegiance to Rome and taught Christ simple, from his memory of the Holy Book. Uncle Avram plunged into his memory of ancient metallurgy and taught the people who gathered at Richmond how to make iron hard enough to use for tools. And weapons.

Father Michael forbade the making of guns and forbade that anyone teach children what guns were. But for hunting there had to be arrows, and what will kill a deer will also kill a man.

Many people agreed with Mother Elouise about the stockade. But then in the worst of winter a tribe came from the mountains and threw fire against the stockade and against the ships that kept trade alive along the whole coast. The archers of Richmond killed most of them, and people said to Mother Elouise, "Now you must agree we need the stockade."

Mother Elouise said, "Would they have come with fire if there had been no wall?"

How can anyone judge the greatest need? Just as the angel of death had come to plant the seeds of a better life, so that angel of life had to be hard and endure death so the many could live. Father Michael and Uncle Avram held to the laws of Christ simple, for did not the Holy Book say,

"Love your enemies, and smite them only when they attack you; chase them not out into the forest, but let them live as long as they leave you alone"?

I remember that winter. I remember watching while they buried the dead tribesmen. Their bodies had stiffened quickly, but Mother Elouise brought me to see them and said, "This is death, remember it, remember it." What did Mother Elouise know? Death is our passage from flesh into the living wind, until Christ brings us forth into flesh again. Mother Elouise will find Father Charlie again, and every wound will be made whole.

Elouise knelt by the Rectifier and carefully set it to go off in half an hour, destroying itself and the time capsule buried thirty meters under the ground. Charlie stood near her, watching, his face nearly expressionless; only a faint smile broke his perfect repose. Amy was in his arms, laughing and trying to reach up to pinch his nose.

"This Rectifier responds only to me," Elouise said quietly. "Alive. If you try to move it, it will go off early and kill us all."

"I won't move it," Charlie said.

And Elouise was finished. She stood up and reached for Amy. Amy reached back, holding out her arms to her mother. "Mommy," she said.

Because I couldn't remember Father Charlie's face, Mother Elouise thought I had forgotten everything about him, but that is not true. I remember very clearly one picture of him, but he is not in the picture.

This is very hard for me to explain. I see a small clearing in the trees, with Mother Elouise standing in front of me. I see her at my eye level, which tells me that I am being held. I cannot see Father Charlie, but I know that he is holding me. I can feel his arms around me, but I cannot see his face.

This vision has come to me often. It is not like other dreams. It is very clear, and I am always very afraid, and I don't know why. They are talking, but I do not understand their words. Mother Elouise reaches for me, but Father Charlie will not let me go. I feel afraid that Father Charlie will not let me go with Mother Elouise. But why should I be afraid? I love Father Charlie, and I never want to leave him. Still I reach out, reach out, reach out, and still the arms hold me and I cannot go.

Mother Elouise is crying. I see her face twisted in pain. I want to comfort her. "Mommy is hurt," I say again and again.

And then, suddenly, at the end of this vision I am in my mother's arms and we are running, running up a hill, into the trees. I am looking back over her shoulder. I see Father Charlie then. I see him, but I do not see him. I know exactly where he is, in my vision. I could tell you his height. I could tell you where his left foot is and where his right foot is, but still I can't see him. He has no face, no color; he is just a man-shaped emptiness in the clearing, and then the trees are in the way and he is gone.

* * *

Elouise stopped only a little way into the woods. She turned around, as if to go back to Charlie. But she would not go back. If she returned to him, it would be to disconnect the Rectifier. There would be no other reason to do it.

"Charlie, you son of a bitch!" she shouted.

There was no answer. She stood, waiting. Surely he could come to her. He would see that she would never go back, never turn off the machine. Once he realized it was inevitable, he would come running from the machine, into the forest, back to the clearing where the 787 had landed. Why would he want to give his life so meaninglessly? What was in the time capsule, after all? Just history—that's what he said, wasn't it? Just history, just films and metal plates engraved with words and microdots and other ways of preserving the story of mankind. "How can they learn from our mistakes, unless we tell them what they were?" Charlie had asked.

Sweet, simple, naive Charlie. It is one thing to preserve a hatred for the killing machines and the soul-destroying machines and the garbage-making machines. It was another to leave behind detailed, accurate, unquestionable descriptions. History was not a way of preventing the repetition of mistakes. It was a way of guaranteeing them. Wasn't it?

She turned and walked on, not very quickly, out of the range of the Rectifier, carrying Amy and listening, all the way, for the sound of Charlie running after her.

*   *   *

What was Mother Elouise like? She was a woman of contradictions. Even with me, she would work for hours teaching me to read, helping me make tablets out of river clay and write on them with a shaped stick. And then, when I had written the words she taught me, she would weep and say, "Lies, all lies." Sometimes she would break the tablets I had made. But whenever part of her words was broken, she would make me write it again.

She called the collection of words The Book of the Golden Age. I have named it The Book of the Lies of the Angel Elouise, for it is important for us to know that the greatest truths we have seem like lies to those who have been touched by the angel.

She told many stories to me, and often I asked her why they must be written down. "For Father Charlie," she would always say.

"Is he coming back, then?" I would ask.

But she shook her head, and finally one time she said, "It is not for Father Charlie to read. It is because Father Charlie wanted it written."

"Then why didn't he write it himself?" I asked.

And Mother Elouise grew very cold with me, and all she would say was, "Father Charlie bought these stories. He paid more for them than I am willing to pay to have them left unwritten." I wondered then whether Father Charlie was rich, but other things she said told me that he wasn't. So I do not understand except that Mother Elouise did not want to tell the stories, and Father Charlie, though he was not there, constrained her to tell them.

There are many of Mother Elouise's lies that I love, but I will say now which of them she said were most important:

1. In the Golden Age for ten times a thousand years men lived in peace and love and joy, and no one did evil one to another. They shared all things in common, and no man was hungry while another was full, and no man had a home while another stood in the rain, and no wife wept for her husband, killed before his time.

2. The great serpent seems to come with great power. He has many names: Satan, Hitler, Lucifer, Nimrod, Napoleon. He seems to be beautiful, and he promises power to his friends and death to his enemies. He says he will right all wrongs. But really he is weak, until people believe in him and give him the power of their bodies. If you refuse to believe in the serpent, if no one serves him, he will go away.

3. There are many cycles of the world. In every cycle the great serpent has arisen and the world has been destroyed to make way for the return of the Golden Age. Christ comes again in every cycle, also. One day when He comes men will believe in Christ and doubt the great serpent, and that time the Golden Age will never end,

and God will dwell among men forever. And all the angels will say, "Come not to heaven but to Earth, for Earth is heaven now."

These are the most important lies of Mother Elouise. Believe them all, and remember them, for they are true.

All the way to the airplane clearing, Elouise deliberately broke branches and let them dangle so that Charlie would have no trouble finding a straight path out of the range of the Rectifier, even if he left his flight to the last second. She was sure Charlie would follow her. Charlie would bend to her as he had always bent, resilient and accommodating. He loved Elouise, and Amy he loved even more. What was in the metal under his feet that would weigh in the balance against his love for them?

So Elouise broke the last branch and stepped into the clearing and then sat down and let Amy play in the unburnt grass at the edge while she waited. *It is Charlie who will bend*, she said to herself, *for I will never bend on this. Later I will make it up to him, but he must know that on this I will never bend.*

The cold place in her grew larger and colder until she burned inside, waiting for the sound of feet crashing through the underbrush. The damnable birds kept singing, so that she could not hear the footsteps.

* * *

Mother Elouise never hit me, or anyone else so far as I knew. She fought only with her words and silent acts, though she could have killed easily with her hands. I saw her physical power only once. We were in the forest, to gather firewood. We stumbled upon a wild hog. Apparently it felt cornered, though we were weaponless; perhaps it was just mean. I have not studied the ways of wild hogs. It charged, not Mother Elouise, but me. I was five at the time, and terrified, I ran to Mother Elouise, tried to cling to her, but she threw me out of the way and went into a crouch. I was screaming. She paid no attention to me. The hog continued rushing, but seeing I was down and Mother Elouise erect, it changed its path. When it came near, she leaped to the side. It was not nimble enough to turn to face her. As it lumbered past, Mother Elouise kicked it just behind the head. The kick broke the hog's neck so violently that its head dropped and the hog rolled over and over, and when it was through rolling, it was already dead.

Mother Elouise did not have to die.

She died in the winter when I was seven. I should tell you how life was then, in Richmond. We were only two thousand souls by then, not the large city of ten thousand we are now. We had only six finished ships trading the coast, and they had not yet gone so far north as Manhattan, though we had run one voyage all the way to Savannah in the south. Richmond already ruled and protected from the Potomac to Dismal Swamp.

But it was a very hard winter, and the town's leaders insisted on hoarding all the stored grain and fruits and vegetables and meat for our protected towns, and let the distant tribes trade or travel where they would, they would get no food from Richmond.

It was then that my mother, who claimed she did not believe in God, and Uncle Avram, who was a Jew, and Father Michael, who was a priest, all argued the same side of the question. It's better to feed them than to kill them, they all said. But when the tribes from west of the mountains and north of the Potomac came into Richmond lands, pleading for help, the leaders of Richmond turned them away and closed the gates of the towns. An army marched then, to put the fear of God, as they said, into the hearts of the tribesmen. They did not know which side God was on.

Father Michael argued and Uncle Avram stormed and fumed, but Mother Elouise silently went to the gate at moonrise one night and alone overpowered the guards. Silently she gagged them and bound them and opened the gates to the hungry tribesmen. They came through weaponless, as she had insisted. They quietly went to the storehouses and carried off as much food as they could. They were found only as the last few fled. No one was killed.

But there was an uproar, a cry of treason, a trial, and an execution. They decided on beheading, because they thought it would be quick and merciful. They had never seen a beheading.

It was Jack Woods who used the ax. He practiced

all afternoon with pumpkins. Pumpkins have no bones.

In the evening they all gathered to watch, some because they hated Mother Elouise, some because they loved her, and the rest because they could not stay away. I went also, and Father Michael held my head and would not let me see. But I heard.

Father Michael prayed for Mother Elouise. Mother Elouise damned his and everyone else's soul to hell. She said, "If you kill me for bringing life, you will only bring death on your own heads."

"That's true," said the men around her. "We will all die. But you will die first."

"Then I'm the luckier," said Mother Elouise. It was the last of her lies, for she was telling the truth, and yet she did not believe it herself, for I heard her weep. With her last breaths she wept and cried out, "Charlie! Charlie!" There are those who claim she saw a vision of Charlie waiting for her on the right hand of God, but I doubt it. She would have said so. I think she only wished to see him. Or wished for his forgiveness. It doesn't matter. The angel had long since left her, and she was alone.

Jack swung the ax and it fell, more with a smack than a thud. He had missed her neck and struck deep in her back and shoulder. She screamed. He struck again and this time silenced her. But he did not break through her spine until the third blow. Then he turned away splattered with blood, and vomited and wept and pleaded with Father Michael to forgive him.

* * *

Amy stood a few meters away from Elouise, who sat on the grass of the clearing, looking toward a broken branch on the nearest tree. Amy called, "Mommy! Mommy!" Then she bounced up and down, bending and unbending her knees. "Da! Da!" she cried. "La la la la la." She was dancing and wanted her mother to dance and sing, too. But Elouise only looked toward the tree, waiting for Charlie to appear. *Any minute*, she thought. *He will be angry. He will be ashamed*, she thought. *But he will be alive.*

In the distance, however, the air all at once was shining. Elouise could see it clearing because they were not far from the edge of the Rectifier field. It shimmered in the trees, where it caused no harm to plants. Any vertebrates within the field, any animals that lived by electricity passing along nerves, were instantly dead, their brains stilled. Birds dropped from tree limbs. Only insects droned on.

The Rectifier field lasted only minutes.

Amy watched the shining air. It was as if the empty sky itself were dancing with her. She was transfixed. She would soon forget the airplane, and already her father's face was disappearing from her memories. But she would remember the shining. She would see it forever in her dreams, a vast thickening of the air, dancing and vibrating up and down, up and down. In her dreams it would always be the same, a terrible shining light that would grow and grow and grow and press against her in her bed. And always with it would come the sound of a voice she loved, saying, "Jesus. Jesus. Jesus." This dream would come so clearly when she was twelve that she would tell it to her adopted father, the priest named Michael. He told her that it was the voice of an angel, speaking the name of the source of all light. "You must not fear the light," he said. "You must embrace it." It satisfied her.

But at the moment she first heard the voice, in fact and not in dream, she had no trouble recognizing it, it was the voice of her mother, Elouise, saying, "Jesus." It was full of grief that only a child could fail to understand. Amy did not understand. She only tried to repeat the word, "Deeah-zah."

"God," said Elouise, rocking back and forth, her face turned up toward a heaven she was sure was unoccupied.

"Dog," Amy repeated, "Dog dog doggie." In vain she looked around for the four-footed beast.

"Charlie!" Elouise screamed as the Rectifier field faded.

"Daddy," Amy cried, and because of her mother's tears she also wept. Elouise took her daughter in her arms and held her, rocking back and forth. Elouise discovered that there were some things that could not be frozen in her. Some things that must burn: Sunlight. And lightning. And everlasting, inextinguishable regret.

My mother, Mother Elouise, often told me about my father. She described Father Charlie in detail, so I would not forget. She refused to let me forget anything. "It's what Father Charlie died for," she told me, over and over. "He died so you would remember. You cannot forget."

So I still remember, even today, every word she told me about him. His hair was red, as mine was. His body was lean and hard. His smile was quick, like mine, and he had gentle hands. When his hair was long or sweaty, it kinked tightly at his forehead, ears, and neck. His touch was so delicate he could cut in half an animal so tiny it could not be seen without a machine; so sensitive that he could fly—an art that Mother Elouise said was not a miracle, since it could be done by many giants of the Golden Age, and they took with them many others who could not fly alone. This was Charlie's gift, Mother Elouise said. She also told me that I loved him dearly.

But for all the words that she taught me, I still have no picture of my father in my mind. It is as if the words drove out the vision, as so often happens.

Yet I still hold that one memory of my father, so deeply hidden that I can neither lose it nor fully find it again. Sometimes I wake up weeping. Sometimes I wake up with my arms in the air, curved just so, and I remember that I was dreaming of embracing that large man who loved me. My arms remember how it feels to hold Father Charlie tight around the neck and cling to him as he carries his child. And when I cannot sleep, and the pillow seems to be always the wrong shape, it is because I am hunting for the shape of Father Charlie's shoulder, which my heart remembers, though my mind cannot.

God put angels into Mother Elouise and Father Charlie, and they destroyed the world, for the cup of God's indignation was full, and all the works of men become dust, but out of dust God makes men, and out of men and women, angels.

KINGSMEAT

THE GATEKEEPER RECOGNIZED him and the gate fell away. The Shepherd put his ax and his crook into the bag at his belt and stepped out onto the bridge. As always he felt a rush of vertigo as he walked the narrow arch over the foaming acid of the moat. Then he was across and striding down the road to the village.

A child was playing with a dog on a grassy hillside. The Shepherd looked up at him, his fine dark face made bright by his eyes. The boy shrank back, and the Shepherd heard a woman's voice cry out, "Back here, Derry, you fool!" The Shepherd walked on down the road as the boy retreated among the hayricks on the far slope. The Shepherd could hear the scolding: "Play near the castle again, and he'll make kingsmeat of you."

Kingsmeat, thought the Shepherd. How the king does get hungry. The word had come down through the quick grapevine—steward to cook to captain to guard to shepherd and then he was dressed and out the door only minutes after the king had muttered, "For supper, what is your taste?" and the queen had fluttered all her arms and said, "Not stew again, I hope," and the king had murmured as he picked up the computer printouts of the day, "Breast in butter," and so now the Shepherd was out to harvest from the flock.

The village was still in the distance when the Shepherd began to pass the people. He remembered the time, back when the king had first made his tastes known, when there had been many attempts to evade the villagers' duties to the king. Now they only watched, perhaps hiding the unblemished members of the flock, sometimes thrusting them forward to end the suspense; but mostly the Shepherd saw the old legless, eyeless, or armless men and women who hobbled about their duties with those limbs that were still intact.

Those with fingers thatched or wove; those with eyes led those whose hands were their only contact with the world; those with arms rode the backs of those with legs; and all of them took their only solace in sad and sagging beds, producing, after a suitable interval, children whose miraculous wholeness made them gods to a surprised and wondering mother, made them hated reminders to a father whose tongue had fallen from his mouth, or whose toes had somehow been mislaid, or whose buttocks were a scar, his legs a useless reminder of hams long since dropped off.

"Ah, such beauty," a woman murmured, pumping the bellows at the bread-oven fire. There was a sour grunt from the legless hag who shoveled in the loaves and turned them with a wooden shovel. It was true, of course, for the Shepherd was never touched, no indeed. (No indeed, came the echo from the midnight fires of Unholy Night, when dark tales frightened children half out of their wits, dark tales that the shrunken grown-ups knew were true, were inevitable, were tomorrow.) The Shepherd had long dark hair, and his mouth was firm but kind, and his eyes flashed sunlight even in the dark, it seemed, while his hands were soft from bathing, large and strong and dark and smooth and fearful.

And the Shepherd walked into the village to a house he had noted the last time he came. He went to the door and immediately heard a sigh from every other house, and silence from the one that he had picked.

He raised his hand before the door and it opened, as it had been built to do: for all things that opened served the Shepherd's will, or at least served the bright metal ball the king had implanted in his hand. Inside the house it was dark, but not too dark to see the white eyes of an old man who lay in a hammock, legs dangling bonelessly. The man could see his future in the Shepherd's eyes—or so he thought, at least, until the Shepherd walked past him into the kitchen.

There a young woman, no older than fifteen,

stood in front of a cupboard, her hands clenched to do violence. But the Shepherd only shook his head and raised his hand, and the cupboard answered him and opened however much she pushed against it, revealing a murmuring baby wrapped in sound-smothering blankets. The Shepherd only smiled and shook his head. His smile was kind and beautiful, and the woman wanted to die.

He stroked her cheek and she sighed softly, moaned softly, and then he reached into his bag and pulled out his shepherd's crook and leaned the little disc against her temple and she smiled. Her eyes were dead but her lips were alive and her teeth showed. He laid her on the floor, carefully opened her blouse, and then took his ax from his bag.

He ran his finger around the long, narrow cylinder and a tiny light shone at one end. Then he touched the ax's glowing tip to the underside of her breast and drew a wide circle. Behind the ax a tiny red line followed, and the Shepherd took hold of the breast and it came away in his hand. Laying it aside, he stroked the ax lengthwise and the light changed to a dull blue. He passed the ax over the red wound, and the blood gelled and dried and the wound began to heal.

He placed the breast into his bag and repeated the process on the other side. Through it the woman watched in disinterested amusement, the smile still playing at her lips. She would smile like that for days before the peace wore off.

When the second breast was in his bag, the Shepherd put away the ax and the crook and carefully buttoned the woman's blouse. He helped her to her feet, and again passed his deft and gentle hand across her cheek. Like a baby rooting she turned her lips toward his fingers, but he withdrew his hand.

As he left, the woman took the baby from the cupboard and embraced it, cooing softly. The baby nuzzled against the strangely harsh bosom and the woman smiled and sang a lullaby.

The Shepherd walked through the streets, the bag at his belt jostling with his steps. The people watched the bag, wondering what it held. But before the Shepherd was out of the village the word had spread, and the looks were no longer at the bag but rather at the Shepherd's face. He looked neither to the left nor to the right, but he felt their gazes and his eyes grew soft and sad.

And then he was back at the moat, across the narrow bridge, through the gate, and into the high dark corridors of the castle.

He took the bag to the cook, who looked at him sourly. The Shepherd only smiled at him and took his crook from the bag. In a moment the cook was docile, and calmly he began to cut the red flesh into thin slices, which he lightly floured and then placed in a pan of simmering butter. The smell was strong and sweet, and the flecks of milk sizzled in the pan.

The Shepherd stayed in the kitchen, watching, as the cook prepared the king's meal. Then he followed to the door of the dining hall as the steward entered the king's presence with the steaming slices on a tray. The king and queen ate silently, with severe but gracious rituals of shared servings and gifts of finest morsels.

And at the end of the meal the king murmured a word to the steward, who beckoned both the cook and the Shepherd into the hall.

The cook, the steward, and the Shepherd knelt before the king, who reached out three arms to touch their heads. Through long practice they accepted his touch without recoiling, without even blinking, for they knew such things displeased him. After all, it was a great gift that they could serve the king: their services kept them from giving kingsmeat from their own flesh, or from decorating with their skin the tapestried walls of the castle or the long train of a hunting-cape.

The king's armpits still touched the heads of the three servants when a shudder ran through the castle and a low warning tone began to drone.

The king and queen left the table and with deliberate dignity moved to the consoles and sat. There they pressed buttons, setting in motion all the unseeable defenses of the castle.

After an hour of exhausting concentration they recognized defeat and pulled their arms back from the now-useless tasks they had been doing. The fields of force that had long held the thin walls of the castle to their delicate height now lapsed, the walls fell, and a shining metal ship settled silently in the middle of the ruins.

The side of the skyship opened and out of it came four men, weapons in their hands and anger in their eyes. Seeing them, the king and queen looked sadly at each other and then pulled the ritual knives from their resting place behind their heads and simultaneously plunged them between one another's eyes. They died instantly, and the twenty-two-year conquest of Abbey Colony was at an end.

Dead, the king and queen looked like sad squids lying flat and empty on a fisherman's deck, not at all like conquerors of planets and eaters of men. The men from the skyship walked to the corpses and made certain they were dead. Then they looked around and realized for the first time that they were not alone.

For the Shepherd, the steward, and the cook stood in the ruins of the palace, their eyes wide with unbelief.

One of the men from the ship reached out a hand.

"How can you be alive?" he asked.

They did not answer, not knowing really what the question meant.

"How have you survived here, when—"

And then there were no words, for they looked beyond the palace, across the moat to the crowd of colonists and sons of colonists who stood watching them. And seeing them there without arms and legs and eyes and breasts and lips, the men from the ship emptied their hands of weapons and filled their palms with tears and then crossed the bridge to grieve among the delivered ones' rejoicing.

There was no time for explanations, nor was there a need. The colonists crept and hobbled and, occasionally, walked across the bridge to the ruined palace and formed a circle around the bodies of the king and queen. Then they set to work, and within an hour the corpses were lying in the pit that had been the foundation of the castle, covered with urine and feces and stinking already of decay.

Then the colonists turned to the servants of the king and queen.

The men from the ship had been chosen on a distant world for their judgment, speed, and skill, and before the mob had found its common mind, before they had begun to move, there was a forcefence around the steward, the cook, and the gatekeeper, and the guards. Even around the Shepherd, and though the crowd mumbled its resentment, one of the men from the ship patiently explained in soothing tones that whatever crimes were done would be punished in due time, according to Imperial justice.

The fence stayed up for a week as the men from the ship worked to put the colony in order, struggling to interest the people in the fields that once again belonged completely to them. At last they gave up, realizing that justice could not wait. They took the machinery of the court out of the ship, gathered the people together, and began the trial.

The colonists waited as the men from the ship taped a metal plate behind each person's right ear. Even the servants in their prison and the men from the ship were fitted with them, and then the trial began, each person testifying directly from his memory into the minds of every other person.

The court first heard the testimony of the men

from the ship. The people closed their eyes and saw men in a huge starship, pushing buttons and speaking rapidly into computers. Finally expressions of relief, and four men entering a skyship to go down.

The people saw that it was not their world, for here there were no survivors. Instead there was just a castle, just a king and queen, and when they were dead, just fallow fields and the ruins of a village abandoned many years before.

They saw the same scene again and again. Only Abbey Colony had any human beings left alive.

Then they watched as bodies of kings and queens on other worlds were cut open. A chamber within the queen split wide, and there in a writhing mass of life lived a thousand tiny fetuses, many-armed and bleeding in the cold air outside the womb. Thirty years of gestation, and then two by two they would have continued to conquer and rape other worlds in an unstoppable epidemic across the galaxy.

But in the womb, it was stopped, and the fetuses were sprayed with a chemical and soon they lay still and dried into shriveled balls of gray skin.

The testimony of the men from the ship ended, and the court probed the memories of the colonists:

A screaming from the sky, and a blast of light, and then the king and queen descending without machinery. But the devices follow quickly, and the people are beaten by invisible whips and forced into a pen that they watched grow from nothing into a dark, tiny room that they barely fit into, standing.

Heavy air, impossible to breathe. A woman fainting, then a man, and the screams and cries deafening. Sweat until bodies are dry, heat until bodies are cold, and then a trembling through the room.

A door, and then the king, huger than any had thought, his many arms revolting. Vomit on your back from the man behind, then your own vomit, and your bladder empties in fear. The arms reach, and screams are all around, screams in all throats, screams until all voices are silenced. Then one man plucked writhing from the crowd, the door closed again, darkness back, and the stench and heat and terror greater than before.

Silence. And in the distance a drawn-out cry of agony.

Silence. Hours. And then the open door again, the king again, the scream again.

The third time the king is in the door and out of the crowd walks one who is not screaming, whose shirt is caked with stale vomit but who is not vomiting, whose eyes are calm and whose lips are at peace and whose eyes shine. The Shepherd, though known then by another name.

He walks to the king and reaches out his hand, and he is not seized. He is led, and he walks out, and the door closes.

Silence. Hours. And still no scream.

And then the pen is gone, into the nothing it seemed to come from, and the air is clear and the sun is shining and the grass is green. There is only one change: the castle, rising high and delicately and madly in an upward tumble of spires and domes. A moat of acid around it. A slender bridge.

And then back to the village, all of them. The houses are intact, and it is almost possible to forget.

Until the Shepherd walks through the village streets. He is still called by the old name—what was the name? And the people speak to him, ask him, what is in the castle, what do the king and queen want, why were we imprisoned, why are we free.

But the Shepherd only points to a baker. The man steps out, the Shepherd touches him on the temple with his crook, and the man smiles and walks toward the castle.

Four strong men likewise sent on their way, and a boy, and another man, and then the people begin to murmur and shrink back from the Shepherd. His face is still beautiful, but they remember the scream they heard in the pen. They do not want to go to the castle. They do not trust the empty smiles of those who go.

And then the Shepherd comes again, and again, and limbs are lost from living men and women. There are plans. There are attacks. But always the Shepherd's crook or the Shepherd's unseen whip stops them. Always they return crippled to their houses. And they wait. And they hate.

And there are many who wish they had died in the first terrified moments of the attack. But never once does the Shepherd kill.

* * *

The testimony of the people ended, and the court let them pause before the trial went on. They needed time to dry their eyes of the tears their memories shed. They needed time to clear their throats of the thickness of silent cries.

And then they closed their eyes again and watched the testimony of the Shepherd. This time there were not many different views; they all watched through one pair of eyes:

The pen again, crowds huddled in terror. The door opens, as before. Only this time all of them walk toward the king in the door, and all of them hold out a hand, and all of them feel a cold tentacle wrap around and lead them from the pen.

The castle grows closer, and they feel the fear of it. But also there is a quietness, a peace that is pressed down on the terror, a peace that holds the face calm and the heart to its normal beat.

The castle. A narrow bridge, and acid in a moat. A gate opens. The bridge is crossed with a moment of vertigo when the king seems about to push, about to throw his prey into the moat.

And then the vast dining hall, and the queen at the console, shaping the world according to the pattern that will bring her children to life.

You stand alone at the head of the table, and the king and queen sit on high stools and watch you. You look at the table and see enough to realize why the others screamed. You feel a scream rise in your throat, knowing that you, and then all the others, will be torn like that, will be half-devoured, will be left in a pile of gristle and bone until all are gone.

And then you press down the fear, and you watch.

The king and queen raise and lower their arms, undulating them in syncopated patterns. They seem to be conversing. Is there meaning in the movements?

You will find out. You also extend an arm, and try to imitate the patterns that you see.

They stop moving and watch you.

You pause for a moment, unsure. Then you undulate your arms again.

They move in a flurry of arms and soft sounds. You also imitate the soft sounds.

And then they come for you. You steel yourself, vow that you will not scream, knowing that you will not be able to stop yourself.

A cold arm touches you and you grow faint. And then you are led from the room, away from the table, and it grows dark.

They keep you for weeks. Amusement. You are kept alive to entertain them when they grow weary of their work. But as you imitate them you begin to learn, and they begin to teach you, and soon a sort of stammering language emerges, they speaking slowly with their loose arms and soft voices, you with only two arms trying to imitate, then initiate words. The strain of it is killing, but at last you tell them what you want to tell them, what you must tell them before they become bored and look at you again as meat.

You teach them how to keep a herd.

And so they make you a shepherd, with only one duty: to give them meat in a never-ending supply. You have told them you can feed them and never run out of manflesh, and they are intrigued.

They go to their surgical supplies and give you a crook so there will be no pain or struggle, and an ax for the butchery and healing, and on a piece of decaying flesh they show you how to use them. In your hand they implant the key that commands every hinge in the village. And then you go into the colony and proceed to murder your fellowmen bit by bit in order to keep them all alive.

You do not speak. You hide from their hatred in silence. You long for death, but it does not come, because it cannot come. If you died, the colony would die, and so to save their lives you continue a life not worth living.

And then the castle falls and you are finished and you hide the ax and crook in a certain place in the earth and wait for them all to kill you.

The trial ended.

The people pulled the plates from behind their ears, and blinked unbelieving at the afternoon sunlight. They looked at the beautiful face of the Shepherd and their faces wore unreadable expressions.

"The verdict of the court," a man from the ship read as the others moved through the crowd collecting witness plates, "is that the man called Shepherd is guilty of gross atrocities. However, these atrocities were the sole means of keeping alive those very persons against whom the atrocities were perpetrated. Therefore, the man called Shepherd is cleared of all charges. He is not to be put to death, and instead shall be honored by the people of Abbey Colony at least once a year and helped to live as long as science and prudence can keep a man alive."

It was the verdict of the court, and despite their twenty-two years of isolation the people of Abbey Colony would never disobey Imperial law.

Weeks later the work of the men from the ship was finished. They returned to the sky. The people governed themselves as they had before.

Somewhere between stars three of the men in the ship gathered after supper. "A shepherd, of all things," said one.

"A bloody good one, though," said another.

The fourth man seemed to be asleep. He was not, however, and suddenly he sat up and cried out, "My God, what have we done!"

Over the years Abbey Colony thrived, and a new generation grew up strong and uncrippled. They told their children's children the story of their long enslavement, and freedom was treasured; freedom and strength and wholeness and life.

And every year, as the court had commanded, they went to a certain house in the village carrying gifts of grain and milk and meat. They lined up outside the door, and one by one entered to do honor to the Shepherd.

They walked by the table where he was propped so he could see them. Each came in and looked into the beautiful face with the gentle lips and the soft eyes. There were no large strong hands now, however. Only a head and a neck and a spine and ribs and a loose sac of flesh that pulsed with life. The people looked over his naked body and saw the scars. Here had been a leg and a hip, right? Yes, and here he had once had genitals, and here shoulders and arms.

How does he live? asked the little ones, wondering.

We keep him alive, the older ones answered. The verdict of the court, they said year after year. We'll keep him as long as science and prudence can keep a man alive.

Then they set down their gifts and left, and at the end of the day the Shepherd was moved back to his hammock, where year after year he looked out the window at the weathers of the sky. They would, perhaps, have cut out his tongue, but since he never spoke, they didn't think of it. They would, perhaps, have cut out his eyes, but they wanted him to see them smile.

HOLY

"**Y**OU HAVE WEAPONS that could stop them," said Crofe, and suddenly the needle felt heavy on my belt.

"I can't use them," I said. "Not even the needle. And definitely not the splinters."

Crofe did not seem surprised, but the others did, and I was angry that Crofe would put me in such a position. He knew the law. But now Stone was looking at me darkly, his bow on his lap, and Fole openly grumbled in his deep, giant's voice. "We're friends, right? Friends, they say."

"It's the law," I said. "I can't use these weapons except in proper self-defense."

"Their arrows are coming as close to you as to us!" Stone said.

"As long as I'm with you, the law assumes that

they're attacking you and not me. If I used my weapons, it would seem like I was taking sides. It would be putting the corporation on your side against their side. It would mean the end of the corporation's involvement with you."

"Fine with me," Fole murmured. "Fat lot of good it's done us."

I didn't mention that I would also be executed. The Ylymyny have little use for people who fear death.

In the distance someone screamed. I looked around—none of them seemed worried. But in a moment Da came into the circle of stones, panting. "They found the slanting road," he whispered. "Nothing we could do. Killed one, that's all."

Crofe stood and uttered a high-pitched cry, a staccato burst of sound that echoed from the crags around us. Then he nodded to the others, and Fole reached over and seized my arm. "Come on," he whispered. But I hung back, not wanting to be shuffled out without any idea of what was going on.

"What's happening?" I asked.

Crofe grinned, his black teeth startling (after all these months) against his light-brown skin. "We're going to try to live through this. Lead them into a trap. Away off south there's a narrow pass where a hundred of my men wait for us to bring them game." As he spoke, four more men came into the circle of stones, and Crofe turned to them.

"Gokoke?" he asked. The others shrugged.

Crofe glowered. "We don't leave Gokoke." They nodded, and the four who had just come went back silently into the paths of the rock. Now Fole became more insistent, and Stone softly whined, "We must go, Crofe."

"Not without Gokoke."

There was a mournful wail that sounded as if it came from all around. Which was echo and which was original sound? Impossible to tell. Crofe bowed his head, squatted, covered his eyes ritually with his hands, and chanted softly. The others did likewise; Fole even released my arm so he could cover his face. It occurred to me that though their piety was impressive, covering one's eyes during a battle might well be a counterrevolutionary behavior. Every now and then the old anthropologist in me surfaces, and I get clinical.

I wasn't clinical, however, when a Golyny soldier leaped from the rocks into the circle. He was armed with two long knives, and he was already springing into action. I noticed that he headed directly for Crofe. I also noticed that none of the Ylymyny made the slightest move to defend him.

What could I do? It was forbidden for me to kill; yet Crofe was the most influential of the warlords of the Ylymyny. I couldn't let him die. His friendship was our best toehold in trading with the people of the islands. And besides, I don't like watching a person being murdered while his eyes are covered in a religious rite, however asinine the rite might be. Which is why I certainly bent the law, if I didn't break it: my toe found the Golyny's groin just as the knife began its downward slash toward Crofe's neck.

The Golyny groaned; the knife forgotten, he

clutched at himself, then reached out to attack me. To my surprise, the others continued their chanting, as if unaware that I was protecting them, at not inconsiderable risk to myself.

I could have killed the Golyny in a moment, but I didn't dare. Instead, for an endless three or four minutes I battled with him, disarming him quickly but unable to strike him a blow that would knock him unconscious without running the risk of accidentally killing him. I broke his arm; he ignored the pain, it seemed, and continued to attack—continued, in fact, to use the broken arm. What kind of people are these? I wondered as I blocked a vicious kick with an equally vicious blow from my heavy boot. Don't they feel pain?

And at last the chanting ended, and in a moment Fole had broken the Golyny soldier's neck with one blow. "Jass!" he hissed, nursing his hand from the pain, "what a neck!"

"Why the hell didn't somebody help me before?" I demanded. I was ignored. Obviously an offworlder wouldn't understand. Now the four that had gone off to bring back Gokoke returned, their hands red with already drying blood. They held out their hands; Crofe, Fole, Stone, and Da licked the blood just slightly, swallowing with expressions of grief on their faces. Then Crofe clicked twice in his throat, and again Fole was pulling me out of the circle of stones. This time, however, all were coming. Crofe was in the lead, tumbling madly along a path that a mountain goat would have rejected as being too dangerous. I tried to tell Fole that it would be easier for me if he'd let go of my arm; at the first sound, Stone whirled around ahead of us, slapped my face with all his force, and I silently swallowed my own blood as we continued down the path.

Suddenly the path ended on the crown of a rocky outcrop that seemed to be at the end of the world. Far below the lip of the smooth rock, the vast plain of Ylymyn Island spread to every horizon. The blue at the edges hinted at ocean, but I knew the sea was too far away to be seen. Clouds drifted here and there between us and the plain; patches of jungle many kilometers across seemed like threads and blots on the farmland and dazzling white cities. And all of it gave us a view that reminded me too much of what I had seen looking from the spacecraft while we orbited this planet not that many months ago.

We paused only a moment on the dome; immediately they scrambled over the edge, seeming to plunge from our vantage point into midair. I, too, leaped over the edge—I had no choice, with Fole's unrelenting grip. As I slid down the ever-steeper slope of rock, I could see nothing below me to break my fall. I almost screamed; held the scream back because if by some faint chance we were not committing mass suicide, a scream would surely bring the Golyny.

And then the rock dropped away under me and I did fall, for one endless meter until I stopped, trembling, on a ledge scarcely a meter wide. The others were already there—Fole had taken me more slowly, I supposed, because of my inexperience. Forcing myself to glance over the edge, I could see that this peak did not continue as a smooth, endless wall right down to the flat plain. There were other peaks that seemed like foothills to us, but I knew they were mountains in their own right. It was little comfort to know that if I fell it would be only a few hundred meters, and not five or six kilometers after all.

Crofe started off at a run, and we followed. Soon the ledge that had seemed narrow at a meter in width narrowed to less than a third of that; yet they scarcely seemed to slow down as Fole dragged me crabwise along the front of the cliff.

Abruptly we came to a large, level area, which gave way to a narrow saddle between our peak and another much lower one that stood scarcely forty meters away. The top of it was rocky and irregular—perhaps, once we crossed the saddle, we could hide there and elude pursuit.

Crofe did not lead this time. Instead, Da ran lightly across the saddle, making it quickly to the other side. He immediately turned and scanned the rocks above us, then waved. Fole followed, dragging me. I would never have crossed the saddle alone. With Fole pulling me, I had scarcely the time to think about the drop off to either side of the slender path.

And then I watched from the rocks as the others came across. Crofe was last, and just as he stepped out onto the saddle, the rocks above came alive with Golyny.

They were silent (I had battle-trained with loud weapons; my only war had been filled with screams and explosions; this silent warfare was, therefore, all the more terrifying), and the men around me quickly drew bows to fire; Golyny dropped, but so did Crofe, an arrow neatly piercing his head from behind.

Was he dead? He had to be. But he fell straddling the narrow ridge, so that he did not plummet down to the rocks below. Another arrow entered his back near his spine. And then, before the enemy could fire again, Fole was out on the ridge, had hoisted Crofe on his shoulders, and brought him back. Even at that, the only shots the enemy got off seemed aimed not at Fole but at Crofe.

We retreated into the rocks, except for two bowmen who stayed to guard the saddle. We were safe enough—it would take hours for the Golyny to find another way up to this peak. And so our attention was focused on Crofe.

His eyes were open, and he still breathed. But he stared straight ahead, making no effort to talk. Stone held his shoulders as Da pushed the arrow deeper into his head. The point emerged, bloody, from Crofe's forehead.

Da leaned over and took the arrowhead in his teeth. He pulled, and the flint came loose. He spat it out and then withdrew the shaft of the arrow backward through the wound. Through all this, Crofe made no sound. And when the operation had finished, Crofe died.

This time there was no ritual of closed eyes and chanting. Instead, the men around me openly wept—openly, but silently. Sobs wracked their bodies; tears leaped from their eyes; their faces contorted in an agony of grief. But there was no sound, not even heavy breathing.

The grief was not something to be ignored. And though I did not know them at all well, Crofe was the one I had known best. Not intimately, certainly not as a friend, because the barriers were too great. But I had seen him dealing with his people, and whatever culture you come from, there's no hiding a man of power. Crofe had that power. In the assemblies when we had first petitioned for the right to trade, Crofe had forced (arguing, it seemed, alone, though later I realized that he had many powerful allies that he preferred to marshal silently) the men and women there to make no restrictions, to leave no prohibitions, and to see instead what the corporation had to sell. It was a foot in the door. But Crofe had taken me aside alone and informed me that nothing was to be brought to the Ylymyny without his knowledge or approval. And now he was dead on a routine scouting mission, and I could not help but be amazed that the Ylymyny, in other ways an incredibly shrewd people, should allow their wisest leaders to waste themselves on meaningless forays in the borderlands and high mountains.

And for some reason I found myself also grieved at Crofe's death. The corporation, of course, would continue to progress in its dealings with the Ylymyny—would, indeed, have an easier time of it now. But Crofe was a worthy bargaining partner. And he and I had loved the game of bargaining, however many barriers our mutual strangeness kept between us.

I watched as his soldiers stripped his corpse. They buried the clothing under rocks. And then they hacked at the skin with their knives, opening up the man's bowels and splitting the intestines from end to end. The stench was powerful; I barely avoided vomiting. They worked intently, finding every scrap of material that had been passing through the bowel and putting it in a small leather bag. When the intestine was as clean as stone knives could scrape it, they closed the bag, and Da tied it around his neck on a string. Then, tears still streaming down his face, he turned to the others, looking at them all, one by one.

"I will go to the mountain," he whispered.

The others nodded; some wept harder.

"I will give his soul to the sky," Da whispered, and now the others came forward, touched the bag, and whispered, "I, too. I, also. I vow."

Hearing the faint noise, the two archers guarding the saddle came to our sanctuary among the stones and were about to add their vows to those of the others when Da held up his hand and forbade them.

"Stay and hold off pursuit. They are sure to know."

Sadly, the two nodded, moved back to their positions. And Fole once again gripped my arm as we moved silently away from the crest of the peak.

"Where are we going?" I whispered.

"To honor Crofe's soul." Stone turned and answered me.

"What about the ambush?"

"We are now about matters more important than that."

The Ylymyny worshiped the sky—or something akin to worship, at least. That much I knew from my scanty research into their religious beliefs in the city on the plain, where I had first landed.

"Stone," I said, "will the enemy know what we're doing?"

"Of course," he whispered back. "They may be infidels, but they know what honor binds the righteous to do. They'll try to trap us on the way, destroy us, and stop us from doing honor to the dead."

And then Da hissed for us to be quiet, and we soundlessly scrambled down the cliffs and slopes. Above us we heard a scream; we ignored it. And soon I was lost in the mechanical effort of finding footholds, handholds, strength to keep going with these soldiers who were in much better condition than I.

Finally we reached the end of the paths and stopped. We were gathered on a rather gentle slope that ended, all the way around, in a steep cliff. And we had curved enough to see, above and behind us, that a large group of Golyny were making their way down the path we had just taken.

I did not look over the edge, at first, until I saw them unwinding their ropes and joining them, end to end, to make a much longer line. Then I walked toward the edge and looked down. Only a few hundred meters below, a valley opened up in the mountainside, a flood of level ground in front of a high-walled canyon that bit deep into the cliff. From there it would be a gentle descent into the plain. We would be safe.

But first, there was the matter of getting down the cliff. This time, I couldn't see any hope of it unless we each dangled on the end of a rope, something that I had no experience with. And even then, what was to stop the enemy from climbing down after us?

Fole solved the dilemma, however. He sat down a few meters back from the edge, in a place where his feet could brace against stone, and he pulled gloves on his hands. Then he took the rope with only a few meters of slack, looped it behind his back, and gripped the end of the rope in his left hand, holding the rest of the line tight against his body with his right.

He would be a stable enough root for the top end of the climbing line; and if he were killed or under attack, he would simply drop the line, and the enemy would have no way to pursue.

He was also doomed to be killed.

I should have said something to him, perhaps, but there was no time. Da was quickly giving me my only lesson in descending a rope, and I had to learn well or die from my first mistake. And then Da, carrying the bag of Crofe's excrement, was over the edge, sitting on the rope as it slid by his buttocks, holding his own weight precariously and yet firmly enough as he descended rapidly to the bottom.

Fole bore the weight stolidly, hardly seeming to

strain. And then the rope went slack, and immediately Stone was forcing me to pass the rope under my buttocks, holding the rope in gloved hands on either side. Then he pushed me backward over the cliff, and I took a step into nothingness, and I gasped in terror as I fell far too swiftly, swinging to and fro as if on a pendulum, the rock wall skimming back and forth in front of my face—until the rope turned, and I faced instead the plain, which still looked incredibly far below me. And now I did vomit, though I had not eaten yet that day; the acid was painful in my throat and mouth; and I forgot the terror of falling long enough to grip the rope tightly and slow my descent, though it burned my gloves and the rope was an agony of tearing along my buttocks.

The ground loomed closer, and I could see Da waiting, beckoning impatiently. And so I forced myself to ignore the pain of a faster descent, and fell more rapidly, so that when I hit the ground I was jolted, and sprawled into the grasses.

I lay panting in disbelief that I had made it, relief that I no longer hung like a spider in the air. But I could not rest, it seemed—Da took me by the arm and dragged me away from the rope that was now flailing with the next man's descent.

I rolled onto my back and watched, fascinated, as the man came quickly down the rope. Now that my ordeal was over, I could see a beauty in a single man on a twine daring gravity to do its worst—the poetical kind of experience that has long been forgotten on my gentle homeworld of Garden, where all the cliffs have been turned to gentle slopes, and where oceans gently lap at sand instead of tearing at rock, and where men are as gentle as the world they live in. I am gentle, in fact, which caused me much distress at the beginning of my military training, but which allowed me to survive a war and come out of the army with few scars that could not heal.

And as I lay thinking of the contrast between my upbringing and the harsh life on this world, Stone reached the bottom and the next man started down.

When the soldier was only halfway down, another climbed onto the rope at the top. It took me a moment to realize what was happening; then as it occurred to me that the Golyny must have nearly reached them, Da and Stone pulled me back against the cliff wall, where falling bodies would not land on me.

The first soldier reached the bottom; I saw it was the one named Pan, a brutal-looking man who had wept most piteously at Crofe's death. The other soldier was only a dozen meters from the ground when suddenly the rope shuddered and he dropped. He hit the ground in a tangle of arms and legs; I started to run out to help him, but I was held back. The others were all looking up, and in a moment I saw why. The giant Fole, made small by distance, leaped off the cliff, pulling with him two of the Golyny. A third enemy fell a moment later—he must have lost his balance in the struggle on the cliff.

Fole hit the ground shudderingly, his body cruelly torn by the impact, the Golyny also a jumble of broken bones. Again I tried to go out to try to accomplish something; again I was held back; and again I found they knew their world better than I, with my offworld instincts, could hope to know it. Stones hit the ground sharply, scattering all around us. One of them hit the soldier who already was dying from his relatively shorter fall; it broke his skull, and he died.

We waited in the shadow of the cliff until nearly dark; then Da and Pan rushed out and dragged in the body of the soldier. Stones were already falling around them when they came back; some ricocheted back into the area where Stone and I waited; one hit me in the arm, making a bruise which ached for some time afterward.

After dark, Da and Stone and Pan and I all went out, and hunted for the body of Fole, and dragged him back into the shelter of the cliff.

Then they lit a fire, and slit the throats of the corpses, and tipped them downhill so the blood would flow. They wiped their hands in the sluggish stream and licked their palms as they had for Gokoke. And then they covered their eyes and duplicated the chant.

As they went through the funerary rites, I looked out toward the plain. From above, this area had seemed level with the rest of the plain; in fact, it was much higher than the plain, and I could see the faint lights of the city fires here and there above the jungle. Near us, however, there were no lights. I wondered how far we were from the outpost at the base of the cliffs where we had left our horses; I also wondered why in hell I had ever consented to come along on this expedition. "An ordinary tour," Crofe had called it, and I had not realized that my understanding of their language was so insufficient. Nor had I believed that the war between the Golyny and the Ylymyny was such a serious matter. After all, it had been going on for more than three centuries; how could blood stay so hot, so long?

"You look at the plain," said Stone, beside me, his voice a hiss. It struck me that we had been together at the base of the cliff for hours, and this was the first word that had been spoken, except for the chanting. In the cities the Ylymyny were yarn-spinners and chatterers and gossipers. Here they scarcely broke the silence.

"I'm wondering how many days it will take us to reach the city."

Stone glowered. "The city?"

I was surprised that he seemed surprised. "Where else?"

"We've taken a vow," Stone said, and I could detect the note of loathing in his voice that I had come to expect from him whenever I said something wrong. "We must take Crofe's soul to the sky."

I didn't really understand. "Where's that? How do you reach the sky?"

Stone's chest heaved with the effort of keeping his patience. "The Sky," he said, and then I did a double take, realizing that the word I was translating was also a name, the name of the highest mountain on Ylymyn Island.

"You can't be serious," I said. "That's back the way we came."

"There are other ways, and we will take them."

"So will the Golyny!"

"Do you think that we don't have any honor?" cried Stone, and the sound roused Da and brought him to us.

"What is it?" Da whispered, and stillness settled in around us again.

"This offworld scum accuses us of cowardice," Stone hissed. Da fingered the bag around his neck. "Do you?" he asked.

"Nothing of the kind," I answered. "I don't know what I'm saying to offend him. I just supposed that it would be pointless to try to climb the highest mountain on your island. There are only four of us, and the Golyny will surely be ahead of us, waiting, won't they?"

"Of course," Da said. "It will be difficult. But we are Crofe's friends."

"Can't we get help? From the hundred men, for instance, who were waiting for the ambush?"

Da looked surprised, and Stone was openly angry. "We were there when he died. They were not," Da answered.

"Are you a coward?" Stone asked softly, and I realized that to Stone, at least, cowardice was not something to be loathed, it was something to be cast out, to be exorcised, to be killed. His hand held a knife, and I felt myself on the edge of a dilemma. If I denied cowardice while under threat of death, wouldn't that be cowardice? Was this a lady or the tiger choice? I stood my ground. "If you are all there is to be afraid of, no, I'm not," I said.

Stone looked at me in surprise for a moment, then smiled grimly and put his knife back in his sheath. Pan came to us then, and Da took the opportunity to hold a council.

It was short; it involved the choice of routes, and I knew little of geography and nothing of the terrain. At the end of it, though, I had more questions than ever. "Why are we doing this for Crofe, when we didn't do anything like it for Fole or Gokoke?"

"Because Crofe is Ice," he answered, and I stored the non sequitur away to puzzle over later.

"And what will we do when we reach the Sky?"

Stone stirred from his seeming slumber and hissed, "We don't talk of such things!"

Da hissed back, "It is possible that none but he will reach the Sky, and in that case, he must know what to do."

"If he's the one there, we can count on having failed," Stone answered angrily.

Da ignored him and turned to me. "In this bag I hold his last passage, that which would have become him had he lived, his future self." I nodded. "This must be emptied on the high altar, so Jass will know that Ice has been returned to him where he can make it whole."

"That's it? Just empty it on the high altar?"

"The difficulty," said Da, "is not in the rite. It

is in the getting there. And you must also bid farewell to Crofe's soul, and break a piece of ice from the mountain, and suck it until it melts; and you must shed your own blood on the altar. But most important is to get there. To the topmost top of the highest mountain in the world."

I did not tell him that far to the north, on the one continental landmass, there rose mountains that would dwarf Sky; instead I nodded and turned to sleep on the grass, my clinical anthropologist's mind churning to classify these magical behaviors. The homeopathy was obvious; the meaning of ice was more obscure; and the use of unpassed excrement as the "last passage" from the body was, to my knowledge, unparalleled. But, as an old professor had far too often remarked, "There is no behavior so peculiar that somewhere, members in good standing of the human race will not perform it." The bag around Da's neck reeked. I slept.

The four of us (had there been ten only yesterday morning?) set out before dawn, sidling up the slope toward the mouth of the canyon. We knew that the enemy was above us; we knew that others would already have circled far ahead, to intercept us later. We were burdened with rations intended for only a few days, and a few weapons and the rope. I wished for more, but said nothing.

The day was uneventful. We simply stayed in the bottom of the canyon, beside the rivulet that poured down toward the plain. It was obvious that the stream ran more powerfully at other times: boulders the size of large buildings were scattered along the canyon bottom, and no vegetation but grass was able to grow below the watermarks on the canyon walls, though here and there above them a tree struggled for existence in the rock.

And so the next day passed, and the next, until the canyon widened into a shallow valley, and we at last reached a place where the rivulet came from under a crack in the rock, and a hilltop that we climbed showed that we were now on the top of the island, with other low hills all around, deceptively gentle-looking, considering that they were hidden behind the peaks of one of the most savage mountain ranges I had seen.

Only a few peaks were higher than we were, and one of them was the Sky. Its only remarkable feature was its height. Many other mountains were more dramatic; many others craggier or more pointed at the peak. Indeed, the Sky was more a giant hill—from our distance, at least—and its ascent would not be difficult, I thought.

I said as much to Da, who only smiled grimly and said, "Easier, at least, than reaching it alive." And I remembered the Golyny, and the fact that somewhere ahead of us they would be waiting. The canyon we had climbed was easy enough— why hadn't they harassed us on the way up?

"If it rains tonight, you will see," Stone answered.

And it did rain that night, and I did see. Or rather I heard, since the night was dark. We camped in the lee of the hill, but the rain drenched us despite the rocky outcropping we huddled under. And then I realized that the rain was falling so heavily that respectable streams were flowing down the hill we camped against—and it was no more than forty meters from crown to base. The rain was heavier than I had ever seen before, and now I heard the distant roaring that told me why the Golyny had not bothered to harm us. The huge river was now flowing down the canyon, fed by a thousand streams like those flowing by our camp.

"What if it had rained while we were climbing?" I asked.

"The Sky would not hinder us on our errand," Da answered, and I found little comfort in that. Who would have guessed that a simple three-day expedition into the mountains would leave me trapped with such superstition, depending on them for my survival even as they were depending on some unintelligible and certainly nonexistent god.

In the morning I woke at first light to find that the others were already awake and armed to the teeth, ready for battle. I hurried to stretch my sore muscles and get ready for the trip. Then I realized what their armaments might mean.

"Are they here?"

But no one answered me, and as soon as it was clear I was ready, they moved forward, keeping to the shelter of the hills, spying out what lay ahead before rounding a bend. There were no trees here, only the quick-living grass that died in a day and was replaced by its seed in the morning. There was no shelter but the rock; and no shade, either, but at this elevation, shade was not necessary. It was not easy to breathe with the oxygen low, but at least at this elevation the day was not hot, despite the fact that Ylymyn Island was regularly one of the hottest places on this forsaken little planet.

For two days we made our way toward the Sky, and seemed to make no progress—it was still distant, on the horizon. Worse, however, than the length of our journey was the fact that we had to be unrelentingly on the alert, though we saw no sign of the Golyny. I once asked (in a whisper) whether they might have given up pursuit. Stone only sneered, and Da shook his head. It was Pan who whispered to me that night that the Golyny hated nothing so much as the righteousness of the Ylymyny, knowing as they did that it was only the gods that had made the Ylymyny the greatest people on earth, and that only their piety had won the gods so thoroughly to their side. "There are some," Pan said, "who, when righteousness defeats them, squat before the gods and properly offer their souls, and join us. But there are others who can only hate the good, and attack mindlessly against the righteous. The Golyny are that kind. All decent people would kill Golyny to preserve the peace of the righteous."

And then he glanced pointedly at my splinters and at my needle. And I as pointedly glanced at the bag of excrement around Da's neck. "What the law requires of good men, good men do," I said, sounding platitudinous to myself, but apparently making the right impression on Pan. His eyes widened, and he nodded in respect. Perhaps I overdid it, but it gratified me to see that he understood that just as certain rites must be performed in his society, certain acts are taboo in mine, and among those acts is involvement in the small wars of nations on primitive planets. That his compulsions were based on mindless superstition while mine were based on long years of experience in xenocontact was a distinction I hardly expected him to grasp, and so I said nothing about it. The result was that he treated me with more respect; with awe, in fact. And, noticing that, Stone asked me quietly as we walked the next day, "What have you done to the young soldier?"

"Put the fear of god into him."

I had meant to be funny. Odd, how a man can be careful in all his pronouncements, and then forget everything he knows as a joke comes to mind and he impulsively tells it. Stone was furious; it took Da's strength and Pan's, too, to keep him from attacking me, which would surely have been fatal to him—rope-climbing I didn't know, but the ways of murder are not strange to me, though I don't pursue them for pleasure. At last I was able to explain that I hadn't understood the implications of my statement in their language, that I was transliterating and certain words had different meanings and so on and so on. We were still discussing this when a flight of arrows ended the conversation and drove all of us to cover except Pan, who had an arrow in him and died there in the open while we watched.

It was difficult to avoid feeling that his death had been somehow my fault; and as Da and Stone discussed the matter and confessed that they had no choice this time but to leave the body, committing a sin to allow the greater good of fulfilling the vow to Crofe, I realized that omitting the rites of death for Pan grieved me almost as much as his death. I have no particular belief in immortality; the notion that the dead linger to watch what happens to their remains is silly to me. Nevertheless, there is, I believe, a difference between knowing that a person is dead and emotionally unconstructing the system of relationships that had included the person. Pan, obscure as the young man was, ugly and brutal as his face had been, was nevertheless the man I liked best of my surviving companions.

And thinking of that, it occurred to me that of the ten that had set out only a week before, only three of us remained; I, who could not use a weapon while in the company of the others, and they, who had to travel more slowly and so risk their lives even more because of me.

"Leave me behind," I said. "Once I'm alone, I can defend myself as I will, and you can move faster."

Stone's eyes leaped at the suggestion, but Da firmly shook his head. "Never. Crofe charged us all that we would keep you with us."

"He didn't know the situation we'd be in."

"Crofe knew," Da whispered. "A man dies in two days here without wisdom. And you have no wisdom."

If he meant knowledge of what might be edible in this particular environment, he was right enough; and when I saw that Da had no intention of leaving me, I decided to continue with them. Better to move on than do nothing. But before we left our temporary shelter (with Pan's corpse slowly desiccating behind us) I taught Stone and Da how to use the splinters and the needle, in case I was killed. Then no law would be broken, as long as they returned the weapons to the corporation. For once Stone seemed to approve of something I had done.

Now we moved even more slowly, more stealthily, and yet the Sky seemed to loom closer now, at last; we were in the foothills. Each hill we approached hid the Sky behind its crest sooner. And the sense of waiting death became overpowering.

At night I took my turn watching, with Pan gone. Technically it was a violation—I was aiding them in their war effort. But it was also survival, since the Golyny had little use for offworlders—SCM Corporation had already made four attempts to get a foothold with them, and they would not hear of it. It was maddening to have the ability to save lives and for the sake of larger purposes have to refrain from using that ability.

My watch ended, and I woke Da. But instead of letting me sleep, he silently woke Stone as well, and in the darkness we moved as silently as possible away from our camp. This time we were not heading for the mountain—instead, we were paralleling it, traveling by starlight (which is almost no light at all), and I guessed that Da intended us to pass by our would-be killers and perhaps ascend the mountain by another route.

Whether we passed them or not, I didn't know.

At dawn, however, when there was light enough to see the ground, Da began running, and Stone and I followed. The walking had been bad, but I had gradually grown inured to it; the running brought out every latent protest in my muscles. It was not easy loping over even ground, either. It was a shattering run over rocks, down small ravines, darting over hills and across streams. I was exhausted by noon, ready for our brief stop. But we took no stop. Da did spare a sentence for me: "We're ahead of them and must stay ahead."

As we ran, however, an idea came to me, one that seemed pathetically obvious once I had thought of it. I was not allowed to summon any help to further a war effort—but surely getting to the top of the mountain was no war effort. Our lander would never descend into enemy fire, but now that we were in the open, the lander could come, could pick us up, could carry us to the top of the mountain before the enemy suspected we were there.

I suggested that. Stone only spat on the ground (a vile thing, in this world, where for some obscure reason water is worshipped, though it is plentiful everywhere except the Great Desert far to the north of Ylymyn), while Da shook his head. "Spirits fly to the Sky; men climb to it," he said, and once again religion had stymied me. Superstitions were going to kill us yet, meaningless rules that should surely change in the face of such dire need.

But at nightfall we were at the foot of a difficult cliff. I saw at a glance that this was not the easy ascent that the mountain had seemed from the distance. Stone looked surprised, too, as he surveyed the cliff. "This ascent is not right," he said softly. Da nodded. "I know it. This is the west face, which no one climbs."

"Is it impossible?" I asked.

"Who knows?" Da answered. "The other ways are so much easier, no one has ever tried this one. So we go this way, where they don't look for us, and somewhere we move to the north or south, to take an easier way when they don't expect us."

Then Da began to climb. I protested, "The sun's already set."

"Good," he answered. "Then they won't see us climbing."

And so began our climb to the Sky. It was difficult, and for once they did not press on ahead and then wait impatiently for me to come. They were hampered as I was by darkness and strangeness, and the night made us equals at last. It was an empty equality, however. Three times that night Da whispered that he had reached a place in the cliff impossible to scale, and I had to back up, trying to find the holds I had left a moment before. Descending a mountain is harder than ascending it. Climbing you have eyes, and it is your fingers that reach ahead of you. Descending only your toes can hunt, and I was wearing heavy boots. We had wakened early, long before dawn, and we climbed until dawn again began to light the sky. I was exhausted, and Stone and Da also seemed to droop with the effort. But as the light gathered, we came to a shoulder of the mountain, a place where for hundreds of meters the slope was no more than

fifteen or twenty degrees, and we threw ourselves
to the ground and slept.

I woke because of the stinging of my hands,
which in the noon sun I saw were caked with
blood that still, here and there, oozed to the surface. Da and Stone still slept. Their hands were
not so injured as mine; they were more used to
heavy work with their hands. Even the weights I
had lifted had been equipped with cushioned han-
dles.

I sat up and looked around. We were still alone
on our shoulder of the mountain, and I gazed down
the distance we had climbed. We had accom-
plished much in the darkness, and I marveled at
the achievement of it; the hills we had run
through the day before were small and far, and I
guessed that we might be as much as a third of
the way to the peak.

Thinking that, I looked toward the mountain,
and immediately kicked Da to waken him.

Da, bleary-eyed, looked where I nodded, and saw
the failure of our night's work. Though none of
the Golyny were near us, it was plain that from
their crags and promontories they could see us.
They were not ahead of us on the west slope, but
rather they stood as if to guard every traverse that
might take us to the safer, easier routes. And who
knew—perhaps the Golyny had explored the west
face and knew that no man could climb it.

Da sighed, and Stone silently shook his head
and broke out the last of the food, which we had
been eating sparingly for days longer than it
should have lasted.

"What now?" I whispered (odd how the habits, once begun, cannot be broken), and Da answered, "Nothing now. Just ahead. Up the west face. Better unknown dangers than known ones."

I looked back down into the valleys and hills below us. Stone spat again. "Offworlder," he said, "even if we could forsake our vow, they are waiting at the bottom of the cliff by now to kill us as we come down."

"Then let me call my lander. When the prohibition was made, no one knew of flying machines."

Da chuckled. "We have always known of flying machines. We simply had none. But we also knew that such machines could not carry a penitent or a suitor or a vowkeeper to the Sky."

I clutched at straws. "When we reach there, what then?"

"Then we shall have died with the vow kept."

"Can't I call the lander then, to take us *off* the mountain?"

They looked at each other, and then Da nodded to me. I immediately hunted in the pockets of my coat for the radio; I could not hope to reach the city from here, but in less than an hour the orbiting starship would be overhead, and would relay my message. I tried calling the starship right then, in case it was already over the horizon. It was not, and so we headed again for the crags.

Now the climb was worse, because of our weariness from the night before rather than from any greater difficulty in the rocks themselves. My fingers ached; the skin on my palms stung with each contact with the rock. Yet we pressed ahead, and the west face was not unclimbable; even at our slow pace, we soon left the shoulder of the rock far behind us. Indeed, there were many places where we scrambled on natural stairways of rock; other places where ledges let us rest; until we reached an overhang that blocked us completely.

There was no tool in this metalless world that could have helped us to ignore gravity and climb spiderlike upside down to the lip of the overhang. We had no choice but to traverse, and now I realized how wise our enemies' plan had been. We would have to move to left or right, to north or south, and they would be waiting.

But, given no choice, we took the only alternative there was. We took the route under the overhang that slanted upward—toward the south. And now Stone took the lead, coldly explaining that Da bore Crofe's soul, and they had vowed to Crofe to keep me alive; therefore he was most expendable. Da nodded gravely, and I did not protest. I like life, and around any turn or over any obstacle, an arrow might be waiting.

Another surprise: here and there in the shelter of the rock the cold air had preserved a bit of snow. There was no snowcap visible from below, of course; but this was summer, and only this high an altitude could have preserved snow at all in such a climate.

It was nearing nightfall, and I suggested we sleep for the night. Da agreed, and so we huddled against the wall of the mountain, the overhang above us, and two meters away a dropoff into nothing. I lay there looking at a single star that winked above my head, and it is a measure of how tired I was that it was not until morning that I realized the significance of that.

Tomorrow, Da assured me, we would either reach the Sky or be killed trying—we were that close. And so as I talked to the starship on its third pass since I had asked for the lander in the early afternoon, I briefly explained when we would be there.

This time, however, they had Tack, the manager of our corporation's operations on this world, patched in from his radio in the city. And he began to berate me for my stupidity. "What the hell kind of way is this to fulfill your corporate responsibilities!" crackled his voice. "Running off to fulfill some stinking little superstition with a bunch of stone-age savages and trying to get killed in the process!" He went on like that for some time— almost five minutes—before I overrode him and informed the starship that under the terms of my contract with the corporation they were obliged to give me support as requested, up to and including an evacuation from the top of a mountain, and the manager could take his objections and—

They heard, and they agreed to comply, and I lay there trying to cool my anger. Tack didn't understand, couldn't understand. He hadn't been this far with me, hadn't seen Fole's set face as he volunteered to die so the rest could descend the cliff; hadn't watched the agony of indecision as Da and Stone decided to leave Pan; hadn't any way of knowing why I was going to reach the top of the Sky for Crofe's sake—

Not for Crofe's sake, dammit; for mine, for ours. Crofe was dead, and they couldn't help him at all by smearing his excrement on a rock. And suddenly, remembering what would be done when we reached the top of the mountain—if we did—I laughed. All this, to rub a dead man's shit on a stone.

And Stone seized me by the throat and made as if to cast me off the mountain. Da and I struggled, and I looked in Stone's eyes and saw my death there. "Your vow," Da whispered sharply, and Stone at last relented, slid away from me.

"What did you say in your deviltalk!" he demanded, and I realized that I had spoken Empire to the starship, then paused a moment and laughed. So I explained, more politely than Tack had, what Tack had said.

Da glared Stone into silence when I was through, and then sat contemplatively for a long time before he spoke.

"It's true, I suppose," he said, "that we're superstitious."

I said nothing. Stone said nothing only by exercising his utmost self-control.

"But true and false have nothing to do with love and hate. I love Crofe, and I will do what I vowed to do, what he would have done for another Ice; what, perhaps, he might have done for me even though I am not Ice."

And then, with the question settled that easily (and therefore not settled—indeed, not even understood at all), we slept, and I thought nothing of the star that winked directly overhead.

Morning was dismal, with clouds below us rolling in from the south. It would be a storm; and Da warned me that there might be mist as the clouds rose and tumbled around the mountains. We had to hurry.

We had not traveled far, however, when the ledge above us and the one we walked on broadened, separated, opened out into the gentle slope that everywhere but on the west face led to the peak of the Sky. And there, gathered below us, were three or four dozen Golyny, just waking. We had not been seen, but there was no conceivable way to walk ten steps out of the last shelter of the ledge without being noticed; and even though the slope was gentle, it was still four or five hundred meters up the slope to the peak, Da assured me.

"What can we do?" I whispered. "They'll kill us easily."

And indecision played on Da's face, expressing much, even though he was silent.

We watched as the Golyny opened their food and ate it; watched as some of them wrestled or pulled sticks. They looked like any other men, rowdy in the absence of women and when there was no serious work to do. Their laughter was like any other men's laughter, and their games looked to be fun. I forgot myself, and found myself silently betting on one wrestler or another, silently picturing myself in the games, and knowing how I would go about winning. And so an hour passed, and we were no closer to the peak.

Stone looked grim; Da looked desperate; and I have no idea how I looked, though I suspect that

Holy • 217

because of my involvement with the Golyny games I appeared disinterested to my companions. Perhaps that was why at last Stone took me roughly by the sleeve and spun me toward him.

"A game, isn't it! That's all it is to you!"

Shaken out of my contemplation, I did not understand what was happening.

"Crofe was the greatest man in a hundred generations!" Stone hissed. "And you care nothing for bringing him to heaven!"

"Stone," Da hissed.

"This scum acts as if Crofe were not his friend!"

"I hardly knew him," I said honestly but unwisely.

"What does that have to do with friendship!" Stone said angrily. "He saved your life a dozen times, made us take you in and accept you as human beings, though you followed no law!"

I follow a law, I would have said, except that in our exhaustion and Stone's grief at the failure of our mission, we had raised our voices, and already the Golyny were arming, were rushing toward us, were silently nocking arrows to bows and coming for the kill.

How is it possible that stupidity should end our lives when our enemies' cleverest stratagems had not, I thought in despair; but at that moment the part of my mind that occasionally makes itself useful by putting intelligent thoughts where they can be used reminded me of the star I had seen as I lay under the overhang last night. A star—and I had seen it directly overhead where the overhang had to be. Which meant there was a hole in the overhang, perhaps a chimney that could be climbed.

I quickly told Da and Stone, and now, the argument forgotten in our desperate situation, Stone wordlessly took his bow and all his and Da's arrows and sat to wait for the enemy to come.

"Go," he said, "and climb to the peak if you can."

It hurt, for some reason, that the man who hated me should take it for granted that he would die in order to save my life. Not that I fooled myself that he valued my life, but still, I would live for a few moments more because he was about to die. And, inexplicably, I felt an emotion, briefly, that can only be described as love. And that love embraced also Da and Pan, and I realized that while Crofe was only a businessman that I had enjoyed dealing with, these others were, after all, friends. The realization that I felt emotion toward these barbarians (yes, that is a patronizing attitude, but I have never known even an anthropologist whose words or acts did not confess that he felt contempt for those he dealt with), that I loved them, was shocking yet somehow gratifying; the knowledge that they kept me alive only out of duty to a dead man and a superstition was expectable, but somehow reason for anguish.

All this took less than a moment, however, there on the ledge, and then I turned with Da and raced back along the ledge toward where we had spent the night. It had seemed like only a short way; I kept slowing for fear we would miss the spot in our hurry. But when we reached it, I recognized it easily, and yes, there was indeed a chimney in the rock, a narrow one that was almost perfectly vertical, but one that could possibly lead us near the top of the Sky; a path to the peak that the enemy would not be looking for.

We stripped off our extra gear: the rope, which had not been used since Fole died to let us descend it, the blankets, the weapons, the canvas. I kept only my splinters and needle—they must be on my body when I died (though I was momentarily conceiving that I might win through with Da and survive all this; already the lander would be hovering high above the peak)—to prove that I had not broken the law; otherwise my name would be stricken from the ELB records in dishonor, and all my comrades and fellow frontliners would know I had failed in one of the most basic trusts.

A roar of triumph was carried along the rock, and we knew that Stone was dead, his position overrun, and we had at best ten minutes before they were upon us. Da began kicking our gear off the edge of the cliff, and I helped. A keen eye could still tell that here we had disturbed the ground more than elsewhere; but it was, we hoped, enough to confuse them for just a little longer.

And then we began to climb the chimney. Da insisted that I climb first; he hoisted me into the crack, and I shimmied upward, bracing my back against one wall and my hands and feet against the other. Then I stopped, and using my leg as a handhold, he, too, clambered into the split in the rock.

Then we climbed, and the chimney was longer

than we had thought, the sky more distant. Our progress was slow, and every motion kicked down rocks that clattered onto the ledge. We had not counted on that—the Golyny would notice the falling rocks, would see where we were, and we were not yet high enough to be impossible for arrows to reach.

And even as I realized that, it came true. We saw the flash of clothing passing under the chimney; though I could make out no detail, I could tell even in the silence that we had been found. We struggled upward. What else could we do?

And the first arrow came up the shaft. Shooting vertically is not easy—much must be unlearned. But the archer was good. And the third arrow struck Da, angling upward into his calf.

"Can you go on?" I asked.

"Yes," he answered, and I climbed higher, with him following, seeming to be unslowed by the wound.

But the archer was not through, and the seventh rushing sound ended, not in a clatter, but in the dull sound of stone striking flesh. Involuntarily Da uttered a cry. Where I was I could see no wound, of course.

"Are you hit?"

"Yes," he answered. "In the groin. An artery, I believe. I'm losing blood too quickly."

"Can you go on?"

"No."

And using the last of his strength to hold himself in place with his legs alone (which must have been agony to his wounds), he took the bag of Crofe's excrement from his neck and hung it carefully on my foot. In our cramped situation, nothing else was possible.

"I charge you," he said in pain, "to take it to the altar."

"It might fall," I said honestly.

"It will not if you vow to take it to the altar."

And because Da was dying from an arrow that might have struck me, and also because of Stone's death and Pan's and Fole's and, yes, Crofe's, I vowed that I would do it. And when I had said that, Da let go and plunged down the shaft.

I climbed as quickly as I could, knowing that the arrows might easily come again, as in fact they did. But I was higher all the time, and even the best archer couldn't reach me.

I was only a dozen meters from the top, carefully balancing the bag of excrement from my foot as I climbed (every motion more painful than the last), when it occurred to me that Da was dead, and everyone else as well. What was to stop me now from dropping the bag, climbing to the top, signaling the lander to me, and climbing safely aboard? To preserve the contents of a man's bowels and risk my life to perform a meaningless rite with it was absurd. No damage could be done by my failure to perform the task. No one would know, in fact, that I had vowed to do it. Indeed, completing the vow could easily be construed as unwarranted interference in planetary affairs.

Why didn't I drop the bag? There are those who

claim that I was insane, believing the religion (these are they who claim that I believe it still); but that is not true. I knew rationally that dead men do not watch the acts of the living, that vows made to the dead are not binding, that my first obligation was to myself and the corporation, and certainly not to Da or Crofe.

But regardless of my rational process, even as I thought of dropping the bag I felt the utter wrongness of it. I could not do it and still remain myself. This is mystical, perhaps, but there was nowhere in my mind that I could fail to fulfill my oath and still live. I have broken my word frequently for convenience—I am, after all, a modern man. But in this case, at that time, despite my strong desire for survival, I could not tip my foot downward and let the bag drop.

And after that moment of indecision, I did not waver.

I reached the top utterly exhausted, but sat on the brink of the chimney and reached down to remove the bag from my foot. The leaning forward after so much exertion in an inexorably vertical position made me lightheaded; the bag almost slipped from my grasp, almost fell; I caught it at the end of my toe and pulled it, trembling, to my lap. It was light, surprisingly light. I set it on the ground and pulled myself out of the chimney, crawled wearily a meter or two away from the edge of the cliff, and then looked ahead of me. There was the peak, not a hundred meters away. On it I could easily see an altar hewn out of stone. The design was not familiar to me, but it could serve the purpose, and it was the only artifact in sight.

But between me and the peak was a gentle downward slope before the upward slope began again, leading to the altar. The slopes were all gentle here, but I realized that a thin coat of ice covered all the rocks; indeed, covered the rock only a few meters on from me. I didn't understand why at the time; afterward the men in the lander told me that for half an hour, while I was in the chimney on the west face, a mist had rolled over the top of the peak, and when it had left, only a few minutes before I surfaced, it had left the film of ice.

But ice was part of my vow, part of the rite, and I scraped some up, broke some off with the handle of my needle, and put it in my mouth.

It was dirty with the grit of the rock, but it was cold and it was water and I felt better for having tasted it. And I felt nothing but relief at having completed part of my vow—it did not seem incongruous at the time that I should be engaging in magic.

Then I struggled to my feet and began to walk clumsily across the space between me and the peak, holding the bag in my hands and slipping frequently on the icy rocks.

I heard shouting below me. I looked down and saw the Golyny on the south slope, hundreds of meters away. They would not be able to reach the peak before me. I took some comfort in that even as the arrows began to hunt for my range.

They found it, and when I tried to move to the

north to avoid their fire, I discovered that the Golyny on that side had been alerted by the noise, and they, too, were firing at me.

I had thought I was traveling as fast as I could already; now I began to run toward the peak. Yet running made me slip more, and I scarcely made any faster progress than I had before. It occurs to me now that perhaps it was just that irregular pattern of running quickly and then falling, rising and running again, and falling again, that saved my life; surely it confused the archers.

A shadow passed over me twice as I made the last run to the peak; perhaps I realized that it was the lander, perhaps not. I could have, even then, opted for a rescue. Instead, I fell again and dropped the bag, watched it slide a dozen meters down the south slope, where the Golyny were only a few dozen meters away and closing in (although they, too, were slowed by the ice).

And so I descended into the arrows and retrieved the bag. I was struck in the thigh and in the side; they burned with pain, and I almost fainted then, from the sheer surprise of it. Somehow primitive weapons seem wrong; they shouldn't be able to do damage to a modern man. The shock of the pain they bring is therefore all the greater. Yet I did not faint. I got up and struggled back up the slope, and now I was only a little way from the altar, it was just ahead, it was within a few steps, and at last I fell on it, my wounds throwing blood onto the ground and onto the altar itself. Vaguely I realized that another part of the rite had thus been completed, and as the lander came to rest behind me,

I took the bag, opened it, scooped out the still-damp contents, and smeared them on the altar.

Three corporation men reached me then, and, obeying the law, the first thing they did was check my belt for the needle and the splinters. Only when they were certain that they had not been fired did they turn to the Golyny and flip their own splinters downhill. They exploded in front of the enemy, and they screamed in terror and fell back, tumbling and running down the rocks. None had been killed, though I now treasure the wish that at least one of them might have slipped and broken his neck. It was enough, though, that they saw that demonstration of power; the corporation had never given the Golyny a taste of modern warfare until then.

If my needle had been fired, or if a splinter had been missing, the corporation men would, of course, have killed me on the spot. Law is law. As it was, however, they lifted me and carried me from the altar toward the lander. But I did not forget. "Farewell, Crofe," I said, and then, as delirium took over, they tell me I also bade good-bye to all the others, to every one of them, a hundred times over, as the lander took me from the peak back to the city, back to safety.

In two weeks I was recovered enough to receive visitors, and my first visitor was Pru, the titular head of the assembly of Ylymyn. He was very kind. He quietly told me that after I had been back for three days, the corporation finally let slip what I had told them when I requested rescue; the Ylymyny had sent a very large (and therefore safe) party to discover more. They found the mutilated bodies of Fole and the soldier who had fallen just before him; discovered the dried and frozen corpse of Pan; found no trace of Da or Stone; but then reached the altar and saw the bloodstains upon it, and the fresh excrement stains, and that was why Pru had come to me to squat before me and ask me one question.

"Ask," I said.

"Did you bid farewell to Crofe?"

I did not wonder how they knew it was Crofe we had climbed the peak to honor—obviously, only Crofe was "Ice" and therefore worthy of the rite.

"I did," I said.

Tears came into the old man's eyes, and his jaw trembled, and he took my hand as he squatted by the bed, his tears falling upon my skin.

"Did you," he asked, and his voice broke, and then he began again, "did you grant him companions?"

I did not have to ask what he meant; that was how well I understood them by then. "I also bade farewell to the others," and I named them, and he wept louder and kissed my hand and then chanted with his eyes covered for quite some time. When he was done, he reached up and touched my eyes.

"May your eyes always see behind the forest and the mountain," he said, and then he touched my lips, and my ears, and my navel, and my groin, and he said other words. And then he left. And I slept again.

* * *

In three weeks Tack came to visit me and found me awake and unable to make any more excuses not to see him. I had expected him to be stern at best. Instead, he beamed and held out a hand, which I took gratefully. I was not to be tried after all.

"My man," he said, "my good man, I couldn't wait any longer. Whenever I've tried to see you, they've told me you were asleep or busy or whatnot, but dammit, man, there's only so much waiting a man can take when he's ready to bust with pride."

He was overdoing it, of course, as he overdid everything, but the message was clear and pleasant enough. I was to be honored, not disgraced; I was to receive a decoration, in fact, and a substantial raise in pay; I was to be made chief of liaison for the whole planet; I was, if he had the power, to be appointed god.

In fact, he said, the natives had already done so.

"Appointed me god?" I asked.

"They've been holding festivals and prayer meetings and whatall for a week. I don't know what you told old Pru, but you are golden property to them. If you told them all to march into the ocean, I swear they'd do it. Don't you realize what an opportunity this is? You could have screwed it up on the mountain, you know that. One false move and that would have been it. But you turned a potential disaster—and one not entirely of your making, I know that—you turned that disaster into the best damn contact point with a xenosociety I've ever seen. Do you realize what this means? You've got to get busy right away, as soon as you can, get the contracts signed and the work begun while there's still this groundswell of affection for you. Shades of the White Messiah the Indians thought Cortes was—but that's history, and you've made history this time, I promise." And on he went until at last, unable to bear it anymore, I *tried*—indeed, I'm still trying—to explain to him that what had happened on the mountain was not *for* the corporation.

"Nonsense," he said. "Couldn't have done anything *better* for the corporation if you'd stayed up a week trying to think of it."

I tried again. I told him about the men who had died, what I owed to them.

"Sentiment. Sentiment's good in a man. Nothing to risk your life over, but you were tired."

And I tried again, fool that I was, and explained about the vow, and about my feelings as I decided to carry the thing through to its conclusion. And at last Tack fell silent and thought about what I had said, and left the room.

That was when the visits with the psychologists began, and while they found me, of course, perfectly competent mentally (trust Tack to overreact, and they knew it), when I requested that I be transferred from the planet, they found a loophole that let me go without breaking contract or losing pay.

But the word was out throughout the corporation that I had gone native on Worthing, that I had actually performed an arcane rite involving blood, ice, a mountain peak, and a dead man's half-digested dinner. I could bear the rumors of madness. It is the laughter that is unbearable, because those who cannot dream of the climb to the mountain, who did not know the men who died for me and for Crofe—how can they help but laugh?

And how can I help but hate them?

Which is why I request again my retirement from the corporation. I will accept half retirement, if that is necessary. I'll accept *no* retirement, in fact, if the record can only stay clear. I will not accept a retirement that lists me as mentally incompetent. I will not accept a retirement that forces me to live anywhere but on Ylymyn Island.

I know that it is forbidden, but these are unusual circumstances. I will certainly be accepted there; I will acquit myself with dignity; I wish only to live out my life with people who understand honor perhaps better than any others I have known of.

It is absurd, I know. You will deny my request, I know, as you have a hundred times before. But I hoped that if you knew my story, knew as best I could tell it the whys behind my determination to leave the corporation, that perhaps you would understand why I have not been able to forget that Pru told me, "Now you are Ice, too; and now your soul shall be set free in the Sky." It is not the hope of a life after death—I have no such hope. It is the hope that at my death honorable men will go to some trouble to bid me farewell.

Indeed, it is no hope at all, but rather a certainty. I, like every modern man, have clung since childhood to a code, to a law that struggled to give a purpose to life. All the laws are rational; all achieve a purpose.

But on Ylymyn, where the laws were irrational and the purposes meaningless, I found another thing, the thing behind the law, the thing that is itself worth clinging to regardless of the law, the thing that takes even mad laws and makes them holy. And by all that's holy, let me go back and cling to it again.

AFTERWORD

"MORTAL GODS"

THIS STORY BEGAN with an essay I started writing once, about how real life has no borders and boundaries, no frame surrounding it the way that paintings do, no beginnings and ends like stories. It occurred to me that artists who tried to get rid of those frames and boundaries and beginnings and endings were making a foolish mistake. First of all, it can't be done—any work of an individual human being *will* have boundaries, both in time and in space, and any attempt to evade that is pure deception. Second, it *shouldn't* be done, because the very reason why human beings hunger so for art—especially for storytelling—is because art, with its beginnings and endings, provides an overlay of order on the chaos of life. Life never means anything, not clearly enough to count on it, but art *always* means something. Its very edges declare that this is inside the boundary and everything else is out.

The essay never got written. Instead, I wandered off into the idea that human life does in fact have one very simple but natural frame: birth and death. So while the mass of human life, taken together, cannot be separated into simple cause-and-effect chains that can be unambiguously interpreted, the life of a mortal being always has definable limits. And after a person has died, then it might, just might, be possible to go about discovering what actually happened within the frame of those two moments, birth and death, and what all those years between might mean.

This speculation would give rise, in the long run, to my concept of a speaker for the dead. In the short run, though, it gave rise to "Mortal Gods," for if it is death that provides the limit that allows life to be comprehended, that allows us to assign meaning to life, then what would this mean to sentient creatures who *could* not die? All our gods seem to be immortal—but wouldn't immortals search for mortal gods?

"SAVING GRACE"

When Kristine and I moved our family from the Great American West (i.e., the part of the country where trees only grow if you water them) to the

Great American East (i.e., the part of the country where trees grow everywhere you haven't paved or mowed recently), one of the biggest cultural shocks was religious television. There just isn't that much of it out west, especially in Mormon country, where our video style is at once slicker and more sedate. So when I saw TV preachers for the first time, especially TV faith healers like Ernest Ainglee, I watched them for hours in horrified fascination.

Of course I knew that the faith healing business was rife with fakery and fraud. But what struck me most powerfully was the deep and desperate faith of those who came, day after day, week after week, to be healed. I wanted to write a story about one of those believers. I also wanted to write about somebody who *really* had the power to heal, and how he would get along with the fakes. When I realized they were the same story, I was able to write "Saving Grace."

That was in South Bend, Indiana, in 1982. I wrote it. I mailed it out. Nobody bought it.

Yet I knew it was a good story. I had read it aloud at a couple of conventions and the audience response told me that it worked, absolutely. So why didn't it sell?

I think part of the problem was that the story was too sympathetic to religion—it wasn't light and satirical enough, and the main characters seemed to be, after a fashion, believers. I don't think the sci-fi markets in those days were ready for that. Also, TV charismatics hadn't yet taken as much prominence in the public eye as they would half a decade later, when every cable system seemed to have a bunch of religious stations, and when the antics of that immortal love triangle of Jim and Tammy and Jessica, and of voyeur extraordinaire Jimmy Swaggart, made these guys household names.

Whatever the reason, I couldn't sell the story. Until, years later, a nice guy and talented writer and editor named Alan Rodgers told me that *Twilight Zone* magazine was spinning off a horror digest called *Night Cry*, and did I have anything he might publish? I *never* wrote horror—at least not in the normal conception of the term—but I did have a contemporary fantasy called "Saving Grace." I told him something about it, and he said, Sure, send it along.

I pulled the story out, thinking to do some major revisions. Instead I found that it needed only some minor changes to be up to speed; Alan bought it by return mail. The result was that "Saving Grace" did finally reach an audience—though I dare say that people buying *Night Cry* had to be more than a little surprised at what *this* story turned out to be!

"EYE FOR EYE"

This story began in my ancient Datsun B-210, a hideously rusted out blue coupe that I had bought from a friend who had pretty well used it up on the salt-covered roads in Lafayette, Indiana, while he got his doctorate at Purdue. The car vibrated so much that after a trip of more than fifty miles I ended up trembling for hours. But it served me well for many years, on trips to Texas, Michigan, Florida, and points in between. I couldn't bear to sell it—I finally gave it away.

All this has nothing to do with "Eye for Eye." I just miss the old car.

I was driving to a convention in Roanoke, Virginia, with my good friend and fellow writer, Gregg Keizer. He had been a student of mine in an evening class I taught at the University of Utah in the late 70s. The class was on writing science fiction, but Gregg never learned anything from me—he already knew how before he got there. I once was so sure that a story of his would sell that I bet him that if it didn't sell within a year I'd run naked through Orson Spencer Hall (the building where the class was held). It took more than a year. I reneged on the bet. But Gregg was very nice about it. And the story *did* sell soon after. Anyway, when I moved to Greensboro to be senior editor at Compute! Books, and we needed to hire another assistant editor, I thought of Gregg, called him up, and asked him if he wanted to apply. He did. He got the job and did brilliantly. He also long outlasted me, ending up as editor of *Compute! Magazine* five years after I walked away from the place.

This has nothing to do with "Eye for Eye," either. But Gregg is living in Shreveport, Louisiana, these days, and I miss him, too.

Anyway, Gregg and I were on our way to Roanoke, and just for the fun of it we decided to come up with some story ideas. Actually, I think I was saying some damfool thing about how a *real* writer could come up with a story idea anytime he felt like it, and make it work, too. So my ego was invested in this, just a little bit. The story idea I came up with was, what if a person discovered he had the ability to cause cancer in other people? What if he had had the ability for a long time, but didn't realize why all the people around him were all dying of cancer?

That was my story—finding out that you had killed people without meaning to. When I actually got down to writing it, of course, I raised the stakes by making it so my hero had killed the people closest to him; I also made him a pretty decent guy. The rest of the story came out of my speculations on how such an ability might arise. I had read a little bit about this doctor in Scandinavia who was trying to promote the body's ability to heal itself by adjusting the electromagnetic field that surrounds living organisms, so I used that to give the story a pseudoscientific veneer.

Because I had thought of the story on the way to Roanoke, and because I first publicly discussed the idea at that convention, I tipped my hat to the folks there by setting part of the story in their town, which has an extraordinarily beautiful setting in the mountains of western Virginia. The rest of the story arose from that setting. What if the gift arose from a bunch of serious inbreeding in a remote mountain community? And how would good mountain people interpret it if they found all their enemies just naturally dying of cancer?

They'd know it had to be either God or the devil doing it, and, given a choice, they'd be bound to settle on God. I decided that they'd consider themselves to be a chosen people, which is why they only bred with each other—but since each generation would have a few kids with more and more intense power to disturb other people's magnetic fields, being their parents would be downright dangerous. So of course, like legendary cuckoos, they'd put them in somebody else's home to raise, only coming to claim them when they'd found out about their powers and had learned to control them.

Add a group of unbelievers who split off from the group, and you've got "Eye for Eye."

I sent the story around when I first wrote it, even though it didn't really feel finished. Everybody rejected it, partly because it was too long; but the nicest letter came from Stan Schmidt at *Analog*, who suggested that he might buy it if the scientific justification were beefed up.

Years later I ran across a copy of the story, with Stan's letter. I had forgotten that it even existed. Looking through it, I decided the idea had some merit, and rewrote it from beginning to end. This time the structure worked better, because I set it up as a first-person account as the boy tried to persuade the unbelievers not to kill him. And, because he had asked for revisions, I sent it to Stan. Alas, he still didn't like it; but by this time, Gardner Dozois was editing *Isaac Asimov's Science Fiction Magazine*, so I asked Stan to send it down the hall to Gardner. Gardner bought it at once and published it. To my surprise, "Eye for Eye" won both the Hugo and, in translation, the Japanese science fiction award as well.

"ST. AMY'S TALE"

Fred Saberhagen had let it be known in *Locus* and elsewhere that he was editing an anthology called *A Spadeful of Spacetime*, which would consist of stories that involved archaeology but did *not* involve time travel. He wanted stories that connected with the past the way science did it, not using the magic trick of a time machine.

I thought about this for quite a while. I loved archaeology—I had begun college as an archaeology major. But how could a story be science fiction about exploring the past *without* using time travel? I came up with a couple of ideas, but the one that interested me most was the idea of anti-archaeologists—people going around *erasing* the evidence of the past. Maybe there had been many high civilizations on Earth in the million-year history of modern man, but each one ended with blood and horror—and with the invention of a machine that could break down human artifacts and return them to their original, natural materials. The machine itself is a pretty hokey idea that doesn't bear close examination, but the human motivations behind the complete destruction of the past are both believable and interesting.

Why, though, did it take a religious bent? In a way, that was a natural turn of the idea, because any idea that can cause such systematic transformation of human life has to end up being religious in character—much the way Communism absolutely functioned as a religion during its first ascendancy in Eastern Europe and the Far East. But there was another influence as well. I was working with some of the great old English writers in graduate school at the time, and Chaucer and Spenser were favorites of mine. I was playing with some of the forms they had used—I started a "Pedant's Calendar" after Spenser's "Shepherds' Calendar," and my epic "Prentice Alvin and the No-Good Plow" contained deliberate echoes of Spenser's *Faerie Queene*. Likewise, I had toyed with the idea of doing a story cycle about pilgrims on their way to a shrine, in imitation of Chaucer's *Canterbury Tales*. That idea went nowhere, but somewhere in the process of planning out this story the title "St. Amy's Tale" came to me. From there, it was an easy matter to introduce a religious overtone, a feeling of holiness and sacrifice to the whole series of events. I thought it made the story far richer and truer to itself.

"KINGSMEAT"

This is the story that readers over the years have found most disturbing and unpleasant. My critics have come up with all kinds of reasons to hate it—including, absurdly enough, a feminist reading of the story in which it was deduced that I "relished" the scene in which a breast is cut off. (One wonders about the mind of someone who thinks that writers "relish" all the scenes they write. Poor bloody-handed Shakespeare!) But once I thought of the idea, it was one of the most inevitable stories I ever told—and one of the most powerful and true.

The origin of the idea was simple. It owed a bit to Damon Knight's classic story that became the *Twilight Zone* episode "To Serve Man." The idea of aliens who eat human beings is as old as sci-fi. But what about a story in which a human being persuades the invaders not to *kill* their victims, but rather to harvest them limb by limb? Would that person be a savior or a torturer? In my mind this idea was linked with the Jews in death camps who were forced into service as body-handlers, fully aware of the slaughter of their own people and, while not directly killing anybody, cooperating with the killers by cleaning up after them. And yet, when you look at it another way, there was something noble in their helpless labor, for as they fed the bodies into the furnace, weren't they performing for the dead those last rituals that are usually performed by family? And wasn't it better that it was done by fellow Jews, fellow prisoners, who mourned their deaths, than to have it done by sneering members of the master race? It's an area of unbearable moral ambiguity—and that's what I strove for in "Kingsmeat."

I think it's interesting that when Gene Wolfe set out to create a Christ-figure in his *Book of the New Sun*, he also made his protagonist begin as an apprentice torturer, so that the one who suffered and died to save others is depicted as one who also inflicts suffering; it is a way to explicitly make the Christ-figure take upon himself, in all innocence, the darkest sins of the world. I didn't plan that out consciously, but I saw it clearly in Wolfe's work and then, by extension, found the same thing happening in mine. That's about the only resemblance between Wolfe's seminal work and my little tale—but I'm glad for any resemblances to the great ones that I can get!

"HOLY"

This story began with a simple enough idea—a challenge, really. Could I write a story that made something as despised and disdained as human excrement seem holy? To accomplish it, I needed to have a point-of-view character who would represent the American reader's habitual disgust for human feces, and then bring him bit by bit to accept another culture's view, until at last he, too, felt that the "meaningless" mission of bringing intestinal scrapings to a particular shrine was worth dying for. Though at the time I wrote this story I would not have stated it so clearly, I was already caught up with the idea that it is story and ritual that give meaning to our actions.

At the time, Ben Bova was buying all the short fiction I wrote. But this story was too long for *Omni*, where Ben was fiction editor, and besides, I wanted to see if I could place a story in one of the prestigious annual anthologies. So I sent this one off to Robert Silverberg for his anthology *New Dimensions*. To my delight, he bought it. I felt validated; and I hoped that my career would get the kind of critical boost that appearing in *New Dimensions* or *Orbit* always carried with them. You didn't sell a lot of copies, but people knew you were certified to be a respectable, *serious* writer of speculative fiction.

Then, to my dismay, the volume that "Holy" appeared in virtually disappeared. It fell into the cracks between two contracts. The *following* volume of *New Dimensions* appeared in paperback before the hardcover edition of the volume I was in appeared, so that my story was in a book that appeared to be outdated—a year old—the moment it appeared. Worse, it never had a paperback edition at all. The stories in that volume were never reviewed. To my knowledge, only a few people in the world ever knew that this story even existed. Its appearance in this volume is, in effect, its first real publication.

None of this, though, was Robert Silverberg's fault—and I thank him again for taking my story seriously at a time when I was being dismissed as an "*Analog* writer" by the literary vigilantes of science fiction. But then, Silverberg has never been one to judge somebody else's work by its reputation, when he has the opportunity to judge it on its own merits. May his tribe increase.